SECOND HAND ROSE

D E Fox

First published in 2023 by Blossom Spring Publishing
Second Hand Rose Copyright © 2023 D E Fox
ISBN 978-1-7393514-4-1
E: admin@blossomspringpublishing.com
W: www.blossomspringpublishing.com

Dedicated to Jake, an inspiration for this crazy story, who will be forever in our hearts and this book.

1

It was early June 2018 when Abigail Hirst packed up all her belongings to make the long journey to Friendship, a journey she had not taken in a while. Grandma had passed away, so it was time to say goodbye. Goodbye to her life in Everett and her job as a reporter at *The Herald*, and to move back, back to Friendship, to Grandma's beautiful house and antique shop, the Second Hand Rose. By her side was her little terrier, Jake, who despite his size could handle just about anything. She fastened him securely in the van and started the long journey home.

Abigail was twenty two years old when she'd left home for the big city lights, determined to be a reporter. Gran never stopped her; she just knew she'd be back when she could. The happy thoughts of Gran kept her going as they travelled, along with Jake's occasional barks at the cows.

After what seemed like hours, they arrived at Gran's home. Abigail had always loved this house. The trustees of the will had left the key under the flowerpot on the porch, so they let themselves in.

Grandma Rose's house was colonial, like the houses in New Orleans were. The architect of Friendship had gone to New Orleans on holiday when he was a kid and the beautiful houses had stayed with him. When he designed Friendship he made a mini version, he said then he would always be on holiday. It was the best of both worlds, Rose had always said. The house was old fashioned with dark furniture everywhere; Abigail had already decided she would sell most of it in the shop. She had also decided she would keep the Tiffany lamps; she loved them and the dining table, mostly because when she was little she'd written her name on it, and Grandma said it was now always hers. None of the table's chairs matched, because Grandma had broken all the original chairs over the years and bought replacements from yard sales. Abigail loved the fact it didn't match, it was so quirky, so Grandma. There was a veranda around the front of the house and Abigail was looking forward to a glass of wine with Jake by her side on a warm evening, listening to the crickets. The furniture on the veranda needed updating, she decided that was her first task – it was nearly summer, after all. "Priorities, Jake," she said looking down at him. She took the box from the car labelled 'kettle', grabbed Jake's bits and bobs, and settled in for the night.

It was early when she awoke. Jake was still snoring next to her. It had been a long journey, so she decided to leave him where he was and start unpacking. It was such a beautiful day; she unpacked as quickly as possible so she and Jake could explore the town and visit the antique shop, which was now hers, a fact that still hadn't really sunk in.

The town was just as she remembered it, nothing had changed in the ten years she'd been away. With streets on either side of a wide road and the mountains in the distance, it was a cross between *Twin Peaks* and Boulder in *Mork and Mindy*. She walked past the sheriff's office, the coffee shop that Martha used to own, the B-and-B, called Friendship Forever that was owned by Sophia Chapman, the bar owned by Geoff Sampson – she loved this town. It was perfect. Jake had so many new smells and new places to explore, and he was happily wagging his tail at every one who said hello to him. She thought to herself, *why did I leave?*

The antique shop was perfect, and the smell of the furniture brought back so many memories, happy

3

memories, sad memories. "I miss Gran," she said to herself. Being here brought that back. She loved old stuff, and now anything old she had a lot of, right in this shop – some beautiful, some not so beautiful. One particular not-so-beautiful piece was a big bedroom wardrobe made from really dark, nearly black wood. She had always hated it, but Grandma said it was special. There were lamps everywhere, but the shop was dark and uninviting. She would change all that. The shop had two big bay windows either side of the front door, so she would take the dark furniture out from them and bring light in. "I can do so much with this shop," she said.

As she looked around, she wondered where the trustee had left the keys, and which one fit the ugly wardrobe. She'd never seen it opened – well, now she owned it she could open it. Just as she started hunting, the shop door opened and there stood Sophia Chapman. Jake wagged his tail and ran over. Sophia looked down at him and said, "Oh." Abigail remembered Sophia was a cat person, she'd had ten of the damn creatures ten years ago and lord knows how many she had now. Jake didn't understand why he didn't get fussed, and then he smelt cats and ran around the shop trying to find them. It kept

4

him busy while Abigail and Sophia caught up.

They talked for an hour or so all about the town, Abigail's job at *The Herald*, and, of course, Grandma. Then, Jake finally came back, probably as he couldn't find any cats, and because he was hungry. Abigail said goodbye to Sophia and said she would pop in the B-and-B tomorrow – without Jake, which went without saying. She closed the shop and started the half mile walk home. It was a beautiful evening and Jake didn't mind walking; Abigail had a pocket of biscuits for him. It was Abigail who was now starving.

2

It was 2001 and Abigail was fifteen. She attended Friendship High School and dated the football captain, Sam Giles; he was the typical All American football star and he loved Abigail. Back then, they thought nothing would break them up. Abigail worked at the antique shop most evenings after school and on weekends. She loved working there and it meant she spent time with Grandma and Grandma was so cool, especially for an old lady – though Abigail would never dare say the word old to her face. Grandma wasn't old, in fact she looked amazing for her age; Abigail hoped she aged just as well. She'd use Grandma's face creams just to make sure; she wasn't going to leave anything to chance.

Friendship was such an amazing place to live. Everyone helped one another – it was like a big family, and no one ever argued or shouted at anyone. Abigail had never seen a fight or raised voice, and never a raised fist.

One day at the shop when Grandma was out getting lunch, Abigail decided that it was time to finally find out what was in that ugly wardrobe Grandma had said was so special. Abigail hunted all over for the keys, but Grandma must have taken them.

Never mind, a screwdriver will do, Abigail thought.

She put the screwdriver into the lock, and *pop!* The screwdriver snapped into two pieces. How could that happen? Abigail hid the screwdriver just in time as Grandma opened the door and shouted, "Lunch, Abigail!"

Abigail excelled at high school; she was in her element. She had straight A's, was good at sport, popular, and she joined in with everything. It also helped that she was dating the school heartthrob. Grandma knew she'd want to move on, but hoped the local paper would keep Abigail fulfilled. Abigail's friends were a strange bunch. Lucy was a computer nerd – she loved gaming and setting puzzles, which she'd give to the rest of her friends to figure out. Monica was perfect. She had beautiful hair, straight teeth, and a perfect figure – and she knew it. But, she also had an amazing heart. Looking like that she should have been a diva, and she was to others but not to her friends. Then there was Roxanne, named after her parents' favourite Steve Martin film and of course the Sting song, which she hated, but Abigail knew when she grew up it would be a talking point and probably get Roxanne a lot of attention from the opposite sex. Roxanne was smart, but not problem-solving smart – she was more street wise, which helped because the others weren't. They were inseparable, and when Abigail was working at the shop on her own they would keep her company. They'd help tidy up so she could lock up on time to get to the coffee shop to catch up on homework and, of course, school gossip.

3

Abigail got ready to go to Sophia's. She couldn't take Jake because of the cats, so she walked him first, told him she wouldn't be back late, and set off on the half-mile walk to town to the B-and-B. Sophia was standing in the bay window when Abigail got there, and waved her to come in. Sophia was like a 50's film icon – she was gorgeous, always beautifully dressed in super high heels, and had long blonde hair which was curled up on top of her head. As Abigail entered the B-and-B, cats came out of everywhere. There was far more than ten – more like twenty. Abigail was a dog person, cats didn't do it for her, so she waded through them and sat down. Much to her dislike, the cats started to climb on her. Sophia saw her uncomfortable demeanour and shooed them away.

"Tea?" asked Sophia. "I also have cake." Sophia presented a carrot cake which was Abigail's absolute favourite, she suggested to Sophia a more generous portion than the modest slither she had initially cut.

Perfect, Abigail thought. She'd walked about four miles that morning already and was starving.

The B-and-B was old fashioned. Most of the furniture had come from Grandma's shop. There were Tiffany lamps everywhere and they made pretty patterns on the ceiling, which Abigail remembered and loved. She'd used to lay on the floor in the B-and-B's dining room when she was younger and watch the colours dance on the ceiling.

"I'm going to have a big open day at the shop," Abigail told Sophia. "Will you help me? I want to invite everyone. We can and have tea, cake, prosecco. What do you think?"

"It's a fabulous idea," Sophia said. "I'll make the cake."

Abigail was hoping she would. "It will be in three weeks, to give me time to tidy. I want to completely change the layout of the shop to bring more light in to make it more inviting, and it will also give me enough time to send out the invitations."

Sophia said she would make and deliver the invitations to help Abigail out, and that she would also put a poster in the B-and-B window, which, due to its central location on the high street, meant you had to pass it going to and from the other shops and cafés.

Perfect, Abigail thought, *I'll ask Justin if he can put a poster in the sheriff's office, too.* Abigail knew he would as he'd loved her Grandma and would do anything to help family out.

Abigail left Sophia busy writing lists, and walked towards the sheriff's office.

"Morning, Sheriff," she said as she opened the door.

Justin Hartfield, the sheriff, was a very attractive fifty-something year old man. Abigail had always liked him, and he'd helped Grandma out. She'd always hoped Justin and Grandma might get together. Justin turned from the desk.

"Abigail!" he shouted. "Oh my God, you look amazing! I'm so glad you're back and running the antique shop, Rose would be so proud."

The sheriff's office had three desks, one for Justin, one for Jared, and a third for a young lady Abigail didn't know.

"This is Shannon Teale," Justin said. "She helps us out with phone calls, filing, and tea."

"Well, mostly tea," Shannon piped up.

"Jared is fishing, he'll hopefully catch something for our dinner later, if we're all lucky."

"Not for me," said Shannon. "I hate fish."

You're in the wrong town, Abigail thought. She said hello to Shannon, who was about eighteen and seemed well spoken and polite.

"How can I help you today?" Justin said. Abigail explained about the big open day and that she needed his help with posters and invitations. He said yes to everything, as she expected. *Things are moving along very nicely*, she thought.

As Abigail left the sheriff's office, she wasn't really watching where she was going and *bang*, she walked straight into Sam, Sam Giles, the love of her life. Great, this wasn't going to be awkward at all. She'd not seen him for ten years. He was the reason she'd left all those years ago.

"Hi, Abigail, you look amazing. How are you?"

Abigail stood there, feeling both anger and love. It was a weird feeling, mixed emotions. The last time she'd seen him he was in bed with another woman, a woman called Mary Watson, two years older and clearly more experienced.

Abigail replied, "Perfect, thanks. Just going to the shop." She paused, thinking. "Maybe it's time for a coffee and a chat, to clear the air." He seemed genuinely happy to see her, but she could sense the guilt and it made it a little awkward.

They walked to the shop, causing all sorts of gossip in the town as everyone saw them together. *That'll keep them going for weeks*, she thought, smiling. Abigail opened the shop door, let Sam in, and locked it behind them. No one was going to disturb this conversation.

Sam explained he was now divorced and that they had had a baby together, a boy called Rowlf. Tragedy struck when he was three months old; he'd disappeared, and they had never found him or a body. That was eight years ago, and they still knew nothing. Mary hadn't been able to cope, she'd blamed herself and she left Sam and the town and went to live in Seattle. Abigail felt awful; she'd had such an amazing ten years since leaving Sam, and Sam had had to deal with all this horror.

Sam asked if they could talk about something happier, which Abigail didn't mind one bit as she could see Sam was struggling to hold back the tears and changed the topic to the big opening. She could see that made Sam a bit happier, but the lines around his eyes were clear evidence of the trauma he had been dealing with. He even wanted to help her out. "Just tell me what you need, I'll do anything to help," he said. He explained he was now a history teacher at the high school; he'd always loved history and after he'd damaged his knee and couldn't play football anymore, it seemed like the natural transition.

After a few hours, Abigail said, "I must go and sort Jake, he's home alone."

"Oh, is that your son?"

"He may as well be. No, he's a scruffy terrier with all the personality of a cheeky kid. Do you want to meet him?" Sam said he'd loved to, but he had tonnes of history papers to mark, so they said their goodbyes and went their separate ways. Abigail walked away with the old butterflies she used to get in high school; she'd never stopped loving him even after all these years.

Abigail walked Jake up to the mountain trail. It was beautiful up there with the stream along the trail, which was just deep enough for Jake to paddle in, and boy did he love to paddle. There were mountains everywhere and dark green fir trees which smelled so amazing. She could see a deer running in the distance and saw a fisherman on the riverbank. She recognised him, it was Jared Lovell.

Jared was the deputy from the sheriff's office, and he and Abigail had gone to school together. He was a bit rough looking, and he'd had a tough childhood – his dad used to beat him, up until the day he disappeared. Most say he'd ran off with another woman, but it was never confirmed, and Jared and his mother never heard from him again. He never sent money or birthday gifts; it was like he'd disappeared off the face of the earth. *Another disappearance*, Abi thought, *but I guess nothing unusual in a town this size over that many years.* Jared never talked about him, and Abigail never brought it up. They sat next to the river as Jake paddled and they chatted for a while. Jared was married to Jane, who now ran the coffee shop since Jared's grandmother had passed away. They'd been married three years and they had an eighteen month old boy named Henry, and Jane was seven months pregnant with a girl. Jared had picked Martha for her name already, after his grandmother. Abigail had always liked Martha, she'd made the most amazing strawberry milkshakes which Abigail, to this day, had never had better than. This got Abigail reminiscing, for some reason, about the day when she and Jake were first acquainted. It was three years ago.

One lazy Sunday afternoon in September, Abigail was sitting in the garden enjoying the early fall weather. She'd been dozing off in front of a crossword puzzle when she'd heard something coming up to the front of the house – it sounded like a dog crying. She'd leapt up and ran through the house to the front door. Upon opening the door, there stood a ginger and white terrier. He was gorgeous.

"Who do you belong to, and are you friend or foe?" she'd asked him, bending down to pat him on his head. He'd wagged his tail, which answered her second question. *But what about the first?* she'd wondered as he looked at her with his big black eyes. "You're beautiful, someone must be missing you."

Abigail had decided to find his owner, so she'd designed a poster – easy enough, as she worked at the newspaper – and put them up all over town. For the next week or so, she'd walked through town, asking if anyone had lost a dog and asking the local businesses to put the poster up. "I wonder where you came from, little boy?" she'd say to him.

Weeks passed and no one claimed him. "I can't keep calling you dog, little man. I think until your owner comes, I'll call you Jake. Is that okay?" she'd asked, bending down to hug him. He'd obliged her with a wag and a lick to the face.

No one ever claimed Jake; Abigail always thought it was fate that they'd met – he'd just turned up on her doorstep. But, he wasn't like a typical dog. Over the years, something niggled at Abigail, but she just couldn't put her finger on it.

"Never mind, Jake, you belong here now. This is your forever home." She hugged him. He seemed to sigh and squeeze into her neck. He was such a lovely dog, and he was hers now. If anyone came to get him, she'd tell them they'd missed out. No one would ever take him away.

4

Abigail had two weeks to turn this dark and dingy antique shop into a haven. Grandma had always had big, dark furniture in the windows, but now it was time to get light into the shop and get it brighter and more inviting. She had hundreds of emails, too, with condolences for the loss of her Grandma, welcoming her to the shop and back to Friendship, and expressing their happiness that the shop was staying in the family's hands.

She had help, of course. Jared and Sam were the muscle and Sophia was busy delivering the invites by hand. Abigail could see posters in every shop window – Sophia had been busy. Jared and Sam shunted the big wardrobe from the window and moved it into the shop, and the light flooded in. Looking at their red faces and out of breath expressions, Abigail realised that the wardrobe must be seriously heavy and probably hadn't been moved in quite some time.

"Jesus, Abigail, what's in this thing? Feels like it's got a Yeti inside!" Sam exclaimed.

"How much better does that look?" she said as they

both moved another wardrobe from the second window. "It looks like a different shop."

She positioned lamps on various tables in the windows and took the big, heavy green velour curtain down from the front door.

"It looks ten times better," Sam said as he looked around.

Whilst all this was going on, Jake slept in his basket, – upside down, as usual – opening one eye every now and then just to check they were doing a good job. Sophia came in with cakes and coffee and they all downed tools.

"Sam," Abigail said, "when we've had a break would you try to get in that ugly wardrobe with the Yeti in it? I've looked all over but I can't find a key, and I've tried a screwdriver but it snapped in two."

After a brief rest, Sam grabbed a crowbar and tried to jimmy the lock. Sam used all his force, Abigail could see his muscles flexing. *Focus, Abigail,* she thought. Then, the crowbar snapped, flying towards where Abigail and Jared stood. *"Duck!"* Abigail screamed. Jared grabbed her and threw her to the ground.

Sam ran over. "Are you okay? I'm so sorry, I could have killed you!" he said, picking her off the ground.

"That was close," Abigail said. "How could a wardrobe lock break both a screwdriver and a crowbar? I never liked that wardrobe. Grandma said it was special. I think it's goddamn ugly, and a bloody death trap!"

It was five p.m. when Sam and Jared left Abigail on her own to finish off the little pretty bits, which unfortunately Sam and Jared were no good at. Jake was finally awake and playing with the spiders that had been woken up when they'd moved the furniture. Suddenly, he stopped playing and stood completely still. He was growling, and all the hairs on his back were up. She'd never seen Jake so angry; he was such a laid-back dog.

"Jake, what's wrong?"

He was staring straight at the wardrobe. The door was open. How could it be open? There was no key. Abigail froze, unable to move. She felt a cold draft pass her legs and shivered. Jake started to back away, still growling. The cold draft suddenly disappeared, and Abigail's body could move again. She grabbed Jake, ran out the store, locked the front door behind her, and ran straight to the sheriff's office. Justin was only too happy to check it out, so she gave him the key and waited with Shannon, who was only too happy to change the subject and talk about their favourite topic: dogs.

When Justin came back twenty minutes later, he said the wardrobe was locked and that he'd checked the whole shop. There was no sign of an intruder. He asked if she wanted a lift home, but Abigail wanted to walk and clear her head to try and figure out what'd just happened. Plus, she had Jake, and he'd proved he could handle himself. She doubted any other man could protect her like he just had.

She started walking home, going through what happened in her head, determined to have another look at home for the key to that ugly wardrobe. She talked to Jake all the way; he's a good listener and, surprisingly, never judges. *What the hell was going on?* She didn't believe in the supernatural, and always poked fun at the dozens of ghost hunting TV shows, but she couldn't explain the events that had just occurred.

5

The next few weeks passed without any further wardrobe related anomalies and before she knew it the day of the Grand Opening was finally here. Everyone turned up to support Abigail; she couldn't believe it. Her old school friends, Lucy and Roxanne, were there, but there was no Monica. She'd asked Lucy where Monica was, but she said they didn't know. When Abigail pushed it, Lucy got uncomfortable, so Abigail changed the subject and thanked them both for coming. It was so lovely to see them both. Roxanne and Lucy looked amazing, and were so happy to see her. Sam came with a bottle and flowers; Abigail remembered how much she'd loved him back then, and how she'd never been in love since. Sad, but true. Was she meant to fall in love with him again? Was it fate that had brought her back? Justin and Jared popped in, too, but they were on duty so couldn't stay long. Abigail was still so happy to see them, regardless. Jake stood near the door with his dickey bow on, welcoming guests; he made a great host.

Everyone said how amazing the shop looked, and that

they couldn't believe it had only been three weeks since she'd moved back. What a difference she'd made.

"It's so much brighter, it looks like a different shop. Rose would be so proud of what you've done," Sophia said to her as she teetered past in her high heels, asking everyone if they wanted cake or wine. Somehow, she managed to carry trays of both – Abigail knew she would have dropped one or both by now if it had been left to her.

Abigail had put the wine and prosecco in the basement because it was the coolest place in the shop. She went down to get some more as so many people were upstairs that she'd run out already after only being open two hours. She was halfway down the stairs when the bulb blew. She yelped, startled by the bang. Jake ran to the top of the stairs to check she was okay. "I'm fine, Jake, don't come down." At that, he went back to his post by the door but kept glancing towards the basement, distracted from his meet and greet responsibilities.

Abigail found the torch on her phone and shone it around the basement. *I must buy more bulbs*, she told herself as she walked around. *Wine, er, two bottles of each should do it.*

As she went to lift the bottles, she felt a hand on her shoulder and the same cold draft from before. This time it was on her face, then on her arms. She shivered. Then, a voice came from the dark, a voice she didn't recognise.

"Don't open the wardrobe."

She turned to find no one. She tried to move, but her legs were frozen to the floor. She tried to shout, but nothing came out. She was paralysed with fear. What was this? What did they want? In the corner of the basement, near the old coal shoot, she could see a figure hiding in the darkness. She tried to shout out, but again: nothing.

"Don't open the wardrobe, leave it alone," the voice said again.

She closed her eyes, hoping it was her mind playing tricks in the dark. When she opened them again, the figure was gone. She didn't understand; there was only one door at the top of the stairs, so where did this figure go, if it was even there in the first place? She walked back upstairs, unnerved by what had happened and more determined than ever to open that damn ugly wardrobe.

She re-joined the party and tried to act like nothing had happened. Jake knew something was wrong and stuck to Abigail like glue for the rest of the day. The open day was a huge success; everyone had a lovely time and thanked Abigail for inviting them. When everyone had gone home, Abigail and Sam were alone, so she told him what had happened in the basement. She couldn't describe the person, and she couldn't even determine their gender. Sam believed her, of course; he'd never known her to be a liar or to fabricate a story just for attention. There was no reason for her to lie.

"We'll do some digging into the history of the shop. Don't forget, I'm a history teacher, I have history at my fingertips. We'll meet tomorrow at the library, if that's okay?"

Abigail agreed. "We'll meet at ten a.m., after I've walked Jake."

She locked the shop up and started home, still determined to find that key and find out who wanted the wardrobe to stay locked and why.

Abigail didn't sleep well that night. She had too much in her head; the open day was a massive success, but the incident in the basement had unnerved her. She was itching to get to the library to try and find some answers – if there were answers to find, that is. She could hear Jake groaning and mumbling in his sleep, and knew she wasn't the only one that was affected.

6

Abigail started the half mile walk to the library with some new information about the shop, which she'd found in Grandma's belongings. She'd been awake all night, so she'd thought she would make use of the time. Upon her arrival, Sam was waiting for her outside the library. When he looked at her, he knew she'd not slept, but he kept quiet; he didn't want to upset her more by saying she looked rough. They walked into the library together, saying hello to Miss Plumb, the librarian, who'd been there for what felt like a hundred years and looked like someone that had worked there that long, too. Old she was, maybe, but she still had a sharp mind. Miss Plumb recognised Abigail instantly and asked how she was, and said she was sorry about her Grandma.

Sam and Abigail found a desk and started going through the books about the town, closely watched by Miss Plumb who, at this point, came over to ask what they were doing. Sam lied and said it was for his class when the break was over, and that Abigail was helping as a favour.

Abigail found a book from the 1890s; it had names of the streets and some pictures, so she started trawling through them. Suddenly, Abigail turned a page and froze. Sam looked up from what he was reading and asked, "What's wrong, Abigail?"

"Sam, that's Rose inside of the antique shop, and look what's behind her – that wardrobe, that ugly wardrobe. What the hell is going on?" Sam looked closely and yes, there was Rose, and next to her Martha, Jared's grandmother.

At that point, Justin appeared. "Hi, Abigail, hi, Sam. What are you two up to?"

Sam replied, "Just some school revision, ready for the new term. Boring, really."

"What about you, Justin, what are you doing here?" Abigail asked.

"Just doing my rounds, see you around." Leaving as quickly as he came, he gave Miss Plumb a wink on his way out.

Later on, Abigail went back to the shop. *There must be a way into that wardrobe*, she thought. *What's its secret, and why did Grandma say it was 'Special'?* Entering the store, she wished she'd brought Jake, but after last time she was worried he might get hurt. She banged against the wardrobe. "Come out, whoever is in there! I want answers!" Nothing.

She went down to the basement, where the other encounter had happened. On the floor was a baby blanket with the initials 'R.G.', but why would a baby blanket be in the basement? Abigail heard the basement door open.

"Hello?" Phew, it was only Sam. "I couldn't let you stay in here on your own. What you got there?" Abigail passed him the blanket. He frowned. "Oh my God. That's Rowlf's blanket, where did you find this?"

"Here," Abigail told him, pointing to the floor.

"Rowlf disappeared with this blanket eight years ago. Why on earth would this be in your basement? Unless Rose took him…"

"Why would Rose take your son? That's crazy."

Just then, they heard a noise coming from upstairs. Sam and Abigail climbed the stairs slowly, apprehensive about what was at the top.

The wardrobe was unlocked again, the doors wide open.

"I thought you couldn't find the key?" Sam said.

"I didn't."

There was no key in the lock, and in the bottom of the wardrobe there was a list of names Sam and Abigail knew, all belonged to friends and family.

"Abigail, my ex-wife is at the top. What's going on?"

Then, a voice came again from the basement. *"You were warned."*

Abigail was too scared to stay any longer at the shop, so she went back home to Jake. She locked the door on the house and checked all the windows before cuddling up on the sofa with Jake. Exhausted, they both fell asleep.

It was six a.m. when she woke up. Abigail decided work was the best way to deal with the previous two days, so she walked over to the shop and unlocked the door. Jake walked right in and settled in his bed. Abigail turned the 'closed' sign to 'open' and sat behind the desk. It wasn't long until things got strange again – the sound of crying came from the basement. Jake's ears pricked up; it wasn't just Abigail that heard it. The crying got louder and louder as Jake's growls got louder and louder. Then, they heard footsteps coming up the stairs. Abigail froze. Who was in here? The front door had been locked. Suddenly, a figure stood in front of her, a dark shape yet again. She couldn't make out who it was.

A cold draft enveloped her whole body, but she couldn't scream, shout, or even run, so she closed her eyes again like before, hoping the figure would disappear.

She opened them to find the figure closer. Her heart was pounding so hard she could feel it in her head. She'd held her breath for so long she was now in pain. She tried to scream once more, but nothing. She closed her eyes again, hoping desperately the figure would go away. But, when she opened them, the figure was running towards her with its arms stretched out.

At last Abigail screamed, but the figure disappeared just before it hit her.

Abigail collapsed on the floor, hugging Jake and finally letting her breath out. Where did it go, what was it trying to tell her? She grabbed Jake and again ran to the sheriff's office. Justin was worried; she was white with fear, and he knew this was real. He walked across the road and checked the shop out again, and again he came back and said, "Nothing."

Abigail walked home, much to Justin's annoyance. With so much going around in her head, she fed Jake and took him on the mountain trail. Watching him paddle made her forget what had happened. He always made her laugh, always had the ability to take her away from the stress of the real world.

7

It was early August when Roxanne walked into the shop. "Morning, Abigail. It's a lovely morning, isn't it? Morning, Jake." At that, Jake wagged his tail so much his bottom left the floor.

"What can I do for you this beautiful morning?" Abigail said as she stopped packing a lamp a customer had ordered online.

"Well, I have something delicate to tell you. You may want to sit." Abigail sat down, extremely intrigued by what Roxanne had to say. "You need to stop digging into the town's past. Friendship is perfect for a reason, and you should just accept it, not question it."

Abigail was shocked. Why would Roxanne say something like this? "Have you been threatened, Roxanne?" she asked. "Have I put you in danger?"

"No," said Roxanne, but Abigail could tell she was lying.

"I think you should leave, Roxanne. I think this is none of your business and whoever has put you in this position is out of order. I don't want our friendship to be compromised, so let's leave it there and forget this happened."

Abigail could tell this wasn't the end of it. She watched as Roxanne started to leave, but, as she was about to step out, she walked back into the shop, closed the door, and ran towards Abigail. Jake started to bark, clearly protecting Abigail.

"What are you doing, Roxanne?"

"You need to stop," she said grabbing at Abigail, going for the throat.

Just at that moment, Abigail could hear someone else behind her. She struggled, trying to force Roxanne to let go, but also trying to see who else was there. It was the figure. It ran towards them, knocking Abigail to the floor, picking Roxanne up, and taking her away.

*

Abigail woke to two friendly faces, one licking her, the other holding her head.

"Jake, I'm fine, I'm awake, thank you."

"What happened, Abigail?" Sam looked really concerned. "You've been out for at least the ten minutes

I've been here."

Abigail explained what had happened. They both looked for Roxanne, walking about the town and trying to call her cell, but to no avail. Confused, Sam and Abigail walked back to the shop.

"Right," said Sam. "I know who can help. I've been thinking about this all night. My old history teacher, Mr. Duggee. He knows everything about this town. He's in a care home, just on the outskirts. We'll go there tomorrow morning."

Sam, Abigail, and Jake walked over the street to the bar, the Welcome Inn. They needed a drink, and more importantly needed to decide what they would ask Mr. Duggee tomorrow.

"Abigail, how are you doing?" asked Geoff as they walked in. "And who's this handsome fella?" Geoff patted Jake on the head, to which Jake wagged his tail.

"Hi, Geoff, this is Jake. It's lovely to see you. Sorry I've not been to visit before now, it's been a little hectic. How are you?"

Geoff was Geoff; he hadn't changed at all. Still mad about dogs, he had a jar on the bar with dog biscuits in. He always served the dogs before the humans, and

Abigail always liked the fact that dogs came first in this place.

Abigail looked down and saw a little Boston Terrier sniffing Jake. "Who's this?"

"Oh, this is Nipper."

Jake seemed happy to see Nipper, and they ran around the bar playing the dog version of tag. Abigail and Sam sat down at the back of the bar and Geoff brought over their drinks. "I'll leave you two love birds to it." He added a wink as he returned to the bar.

Abigail didn't have romance on her mind, she needed answers.

"Alright, I'll pick you up at nine a.m. tomorrow," Sam said, nearly drinking his beer in one mouthful. "If anyone knows what's going on around here, it will be Mr. Duggee."

Unfortunately, as Sam explained, Mr. Duggee had terminal cancer and didn't have long left to live. Sam hoped they wouldn't upset him when they turned up tomorrow; he admired and respected Mr. Duggee, he was the one who pushed him into teaching when he injured his knee.

Geoff brought two more drinks over. "Looks like a

two-drink chat," he said as he placed the drinks on the table. Abigail looked over to where Jake and Nipper were playing. They had stopped playing tag and were now like March hares on their back legs. Jake had the upper hand slightly, as he was taller. It made Abigail laugh; Jake was always a happy distraction.

They finished their drinks and Abigail told Jake to say goodbye to his new friend. "Thanks, Geoff, see you soon."

They left the bar and went their separate ways. "See you tomorrow, Sam," she said as they parted. Abigail walked home, unaware of watchful eyes following her every move, unaware that, as soon as she left the bar, Geoff had called a meeting, a meeting with Justin and a third person.

*

The next day, Sam was early. Abigail didn't mind, she had already walked Jake and was ready to go. She had a list of questions for Mr. Duggee; even if he only answered half of them, they'd be better off.

It was a twenty minute drive to the care home. The

drive was very quiet; Sam and Abigail didn't say much as they each had too much on their minds.

As Sam pulled into the car park, Abigail said, "I'd like to live here." The building was like a beautiful stately home, looking more like it was from *Downton Abbey* compared to the drab, featureless buildings normally associated with these places. They got out of the car and walked towards the front door where a large, male nurse met them.

"Hi, Sam," he said. "It's been a while. Who's this?"

"Abigail, this is Monty. Monty, this is Abigail, Rose's granddaughter."

"Oh, yes, I can see the resemblance now you mention it. Have you come to visit Mr. Duggee? He'll be so pleased to see you, I'll take you through." Monty walked them through two massive communal rooms full of elderly people either playing cards or checkers. In the second one he stopped and pointed to the corner. There sat an elderly man, old before his time, Abigail thought. "There you go, Sam, I'll bring some tea," Monty said, and off he went back across the room to a little kitchen.

Sam sat next to Mr. Duggee, who suddenly lit up. "Sam, I'm so glad you're here, it's been too long."

Sam explained why they were there and what had happened since Abigail had come back into town. Mr. Duggee didn't look surprised. In fact, in didn't respond at all, which Abigail thought was strange.

Mr. Duggee leaned towards them. "You need to stop digging. This town is run by an evil man, and if you do what you're told, you'll be fine. I spoke up, and look what's happened to me. I haven't got long. If you try to leave and he doesn't want you to, he takes something away from you."

"Who else knows about this?" Sam asked.

Mr. Duggee started to feel uncomfortable and looked around nervously as though he was trying to get the attention of someone. Monty came over and saw Mr. Duggee was clearly struggling to respond.

"Sorry, Sam," said Monty. "Mr. Duggee is tired, maybe best to come back in a couple of days. He needs his rest."

"See you soon, sir, make sure you rest," Sam said as Mr. Duggee was wheeled away. Abigail just stared at Sam, mostly in shock but also in disbelief. Was this the gibbering of a terminally ill man on strong medication, or a desperate warning to prevent any further incidents?

They walked to the car in silence and drove back to town. Abigail asked Sam to drop her at home so she could pick Jake up and walk back to the shop to keep busy – that would take her mind off what she had just heard.

She decided to clean the shop from top to bottom, as the disadvantage of selling antiques was dust. The afternoon quickly disappeared, and she looked around admirably at the shop which now looked spotless. It was nearly five when Sam came over to the shop unannounced. "Do you fancy dinner? I'm cooking."

This took her by surprise a little, and her heart skipped a beat at the thought of spending an evening with Sam. *Get a hold of yourself, you're not a teenager anymore,* she told herself. She did still have mixed emotions because of the past, but tried to hide this as best she could. "That would be lovely. I just need to get Jake some food from the grocery shop as we pass." They all walked to the grocery shop, bought wine and other supplies, and then carried on to Sam's.

Sam lived on the opposite end of the town to Abigail in a lovely house which he'd kept in the divorce. Mary had said she didn't want it, as it had too many bad memories of Rowlf. Sam cooked dinner whilst they chatted, unaware of events across town. Things were taking a turn for the worst.

8

Back in the care home, Mr. Duggee had had his dinner and was just settling in his armchair for the evening when he heard something, or someone, in his room. He reached for the lamp, switching it on. Nothing happened. He knew he was here, that he had heard everything that was said earlier. He could make out a figure in the corner moving slowly towards him. Mr. Duggee tried to move, but was frozen with fear. He knew what the figure was capable of. He'd seen him kill before. He'd seen Rowlf's death; a death that had haunted him, haunted his dreams. The figure moved forward. He felt a hand touch his head.

"I told you what would happen if you told anyone about me."

"I'm sorry!" Mr. Duggee cried out. "I'll tell them I made it all up! The drugs were talking!"

"It's too late."

Mr. Duggee somehow managed to get out of his armchair and into the wheelchair. Adrenaline pushed him to get out of the room and down the hall to the elevator. He knew he needed to get away.   The elevator door opened. He wheeled himself in, pressed the button for the basement, and started to descend.

The elevator stopped. The lights went out. He tried to press the basement number again, but nothing. He tried the emergency button, and nothing again. He was stuck, and at the mercy of the figure.

The lights started to flicker. Mr. Duggee looked down at his hands; they were grey and gnarled. The skin was hanging off his bones and all the life was being drained from his body, bit by bit. He looked at his arms. They were now saggy, his skin loose all over his skeleton. He screamed as his eyes popped from his head – he could feel them land on his knee. His whole-body was limp and slowly being sucked of life. His brain finally gave up as the last bit of juice was taken by the figure.

Death had finally taken Mr. Duggee.

The elevator doors opened. Nurse Heather screamed.

9

Justin and Jared arrived at the care home at three a.m.
Monty had made coffee for everyone; it was going to be a
long night. Justin asked Jared to talk to the nurse who had
found Mr. Duggee. She was being comforted by Mrs.
Bennett, who had been the owner of the care home for
about thirty years and had seen everything in her time –
or so she thought. Justin went straight to the elevator. The
sight of Mr. Duggee's body shocked him, even though he
knew exactly what and who had done this. All the other
deaths had been hidden, covered up to some extent, but
this was different. This was public. He couldn't cover this
one up, the state police or even the feds might get
involved.

Jared finished interviewing Heather and went over to
Justin. "Oh my God," he said, turning away. "What could
have done that? It's inhuman."

Justin asked Jared to wait for the coroner outside and
show him to where the body was. It got him out the way,
both because the body was so horrific and because Justin
needed to address the crime scene.

"The coroner is here, Justin," Jared said about thirty minutes later. Dr Gregson was the county coroner – Friendship didn't have one of their own, and that's why Justin knew he couldn't cover this one up; he just needed to change the evidence a little.

*

Across town, Abigail woke up next to Sam. It had been a long time since they'd spent the night together. She remembered Sam was so loving and caring. All the heartache disappeared, and it was time to put the past behind them and look to their future together. Jake was asleep on the landing when she went downstairs to make coffee. She was sat in the dining room drinking her coffee when Sam walked in.

"Good morning," Sam said. "How did you sleep? I imagine not as good as Jake. He can really snore for such a little dog." At hearing his name, Jake bounced downstairs with his usual three-legged approach and ran into the dining room to see Abigail.

There was a knock at the door. Jared was standing there, shaking.

"Come in, Jared, you look like you need a coffee," Sam said.

"Thanks, Sam," Jared said. He entered, and stood in the hallway awkwardly, looking like he was fighting a battle in his mind. "There's been a murder at the care home. Mr. Duggee is dead," he spat out. "The life had been drained out of him. He was killed in the night and one of the nurses found him in the elevator. The county coroner has taken him to do an autopsy, but there wasn't much of a body left to do an autopsy on."

"How awful," Abigail said, "we only spoke to him yesterday. I wanted to know more about the town and the antique shop. He mentioned the town was run by someone evil and that we shouldn't ask any more questions. Was he killed because we were digging around? Oh my God, Sam, it's our fault. We got him killed. We need to tell Justin."

Sam stumbled to find a chair and sat down. The shock of Mr. Duggee's death clearly affected him, as he was not just a mentor but a dear friend and father figure.

When Sam and Abigail got to the sheriff's office, Justin was outside talking to Geoff. "Morning, you two," Geoff said. "I'll see you later, Justin." With that, Geoff walked away towards the bar.

"Justin, we have something to tell you. It's our fault Mr. Duggee was killed. We were asking questions about the town and the antique shop yesterday, and he warned us to stop digging, we got him killed."

"No, you didn't," Justin said. "There have been other deaths like this in the past. The killer targets the elderly or people who haven't got long left and takes all their savings."

"How does he drain the body of all fluids, though?" Abigail asked.

The sheriff stared at her. "How do you know that, Abigail?" Justin asked. "That information hasn't been released."

"Sorry, look at the time, must go, I have to open the shop." Abigail rushed off closely followed by Sam.

10

It was 1891. Rose was fifty and she was in love with Justin Hartfield, and he felt the same. The town of Friendship was growing, they had some lovely families moving in and the antique shop was doing well. Justin, the sheriff, didn't have much crime to solve – just a few disagreements, nothing major. Rose had bought a beautiful house about half a mile from town, just close enough away from busy bodies, as Rose and Justin were not married and didn't intend to be.

One night, whilst they were reading, they heard a commotion just outside their house. It was two of their neighbours; they'd found a man nearly dead from exposure whilst they were fishing in the mountains. Rose told them to bring him in and put him in the guest bedroom; she would tend to him and get him back to full health. He was a strange looking man – his dark, charred looking skin seemed to hang off his bones. He didn't say much, just kept thanking Rose and saying she would be rewarded when he was fully recovered.

Weeks passed, and the stranger still didn't reveal his

name or the reason why he'd been in the mountains in such dreadful weather. Rose and Justin suspected he was a criminal, running from the law, but they didn't, or wouldn't, give him away – they didn't have any reason to think he was bad, as he'd never shown any anger or violence towards either of them. After six weeks, the stranger was recovered, maybe not fully but enough that he could leave the house and go for a walk. Rose showed him around town. He liked Friendship very much and asked if he could stay. Rose said she would really like that, and that she'd find him somewhere to live – maybe he could even help her in the shop. Another two weeks passed and the stranger, who Rose had named Al, had gone out for the evening to the Welcome Inn with Justin. On the way home there had been a fight, so Justin told Al to go home alone. About an hour later, when Justin had sorted out the fight, he went home only to find that Al hadn't returned yet. Rose was worried that something had happened to him; maybe he'd left town without saying goodbye, but he'd seemed so happy and had said he wanted to stay.

The next morning, Rose and Justin awoke to screams coming from next door. They ran out to the street to see their neighbour's wife holding their two month old baby in her arms. The life had been drained from the child; it was dead. Justin took the baby, wrapped it in a blanket, and took it to the doctors where they called the county coroner.

Rose walked back into the house. There was someone sat at the dining table; it was Al.

"Where have you been, Al?" she said. "Did you hear what happened?"

"I could make you rich, Rose," he said. "You just have to keep my secret and Friendship could be the perfect town. You only have to trust me and do as I say."

"It was you, wasn't it? How could you!" Rose was crying.

"I need to feed, and babies are the best and easiest food I can get. I only need to feed once or twice a year, it's not much. I can take the weak, the useless ones who have no purpose in this perfect town."

Rose listened as Al explained; he was many centuries old and had travelled from town to town, cleaning up the weak and the people who didn't want to make their town great. Every town had its fair share of wasters and spongers that never contributed; they just always caused problems, and it was Al that culled. Rose shivered at Al's stories; they were gruesome, but always seemed almost justified.

Just then, Justin came home. "Hi, Al, glad you're okay. Rose, what's wrong?"

Rose and Al explained it all again. Justin was disgusted, but realised that if he and Rose took the information to the authorities that Al would do to them what he'd done to the baby.

"While I stay in your town, you will never age and never die. It's a small price to pay for immortality." They knew that they had to hide Al's identity and pretend he had left the town. "I'll hide in the shop," Al said.

"But, where?" Rose said.

"That lovely wardrobe will do. We can push it against the back wall near the counter, and I can use my portal to come and go as I please."

It's perfect, Rose thought. She and Justin could have their privacy back, and Al could live in the shop.

"This town will be perfect," Al said as he packed up his clothes and Justin got the keys for the shop. Al had found another town to feed on. His plan had worked again.

'Portal' was Al's word, but Rose didn't know what exactly he meant. She just knew he came and went, but didn't know where, when or how. He just had the ability to disappear. His origins were still very much a mystery, and he was certainly not forthcoming with that information. Rose didn't press him on the matter, as she thought the less she knew, the better. Her conscience was already struggling with the hideous secret.

11

Dr Gregson looked at the shrivelled-up corpse in front of him. He'd never seen anything like it, he didn't even know where to start. He Skyped his colleague so he could watch and chip in when he started to run out of ideas; *two heads are better than one*, he thought.

"Hi, Dr Watson," said Gregson.

"What the hell happened here? It's a mess."

Just then, the connection was lost, and the lights started to flicker. *Bloody generator*, Gregson thought. He suddenly felt cold; he could see his breath as he walked along the corridor towards the generator room. He opened the door – the generator was working perfectly. "What's going on?" he said to himself as he closed the door. He turned and was suddenly shocked by a figure standing in the morgue. "Hello," he shouted. "You can't be in here."

The figure didn't turn or move, so Gregson shouted again. This time, he got the figure's attention. As he turned, Gregson gasped in horror. The figure had no face, no features at all. Gregson ran to the elevator and pressed the 'open' button with urgency. Nothing. The elevator didn't move. From the basement, he ran towards the stairs, opened the door, and started up the stairs, looking behind him to see if the figure was following. He stumbled and fell on the next flight of stairs. The lights started to flicker. The figure was now in front of him. He got up and started to move backward. "Who are you?" Gregson shouted.

The figure lunged towards him, grabbing his throat. The creature reached into his mouth and pulled at his tongue, ripping it out as if it was tissue paper.

"Now you can't tell anyone."

As the figure ate his tongue, wiping away the blood as it dribbled down his chin, he disappeared back into the darkness. The power turned back on.

"Dr Gregson?" shouted Dr Watson. There was no response. He became worried; it had been an hour since the connection had dropped, and now it was restored both his colleague and the corpse were missing. He called the police – he was worried that the local sheriff couldn't handle this situation. It needed someone more used to this type of crime, someone from out of town but who was near enough to react quickly. He called Lieutenant Kane, who he'd worked with before on another weird case about ten years ago. This was right up his street.

*

Lieutenant Kane knew when he walked into the morgue that he'd find trouble. He was only called when there was trouble. He saw blood along the corridor and drew his gun; the attacker might still be about. Slowly, he walked into each room, pushing the door back as far as he could. The attacker could be hiding anywhere. Suddenly, he saw Dr Gregson on the floor covered in blood. He radioed for an ambulance.

"Dr Gregson, help is on the way, you'll soon be at the hospital," Kane reassured.

Lieutenant Kane knew exactly what he had here. He sat with the doctor until the paramedics came; he didn't want to leave him, as he could tell he was scared and clearly in pain.

"Who would have done such an awful thing?" he muttered.

The paramedics came within twenty minutes and Lieutenant Kane left them to help the doctor. He needed to make sure the attacker wasn't still here. There were now about thirty officers in the morgue, all checking for the attacker and for the body of Mr. Duggee.

"We've found nothing, sir," said officer McNeill. "There's a laptop on in the morgue; it looks like Dr Gregson was Skyping someone when he was attacked."

"Must be Dr Watson, he's the one who called it in." Lieutenant Kane walked over to the laptop. "Dr Watson, are you still there? It's Lieutenant Kane. Did you see anything?"

"No, nothing," Dr Watson said. "Is Dr Gregson hurt? Everything went dark for about sixty minutes, then when the lights came back on, Mr. Duggee's body had gone. I panicked and called you."

"You did the right thing, Dr Watson," Lieutenant Kane assured him. "We'll be in touch. Dr Gregson has been taken to hospital. He will need a friendly face when he comes out of surgery."

12

Things had become tense between Rose and Justin since the stranger had arrived. They both knew they needed to get rid of him, but he could hear everything, so they had to be really careful. The stranger (they'd stopped calling him Al, as this made him human, and he was far from human) wanted Rose to bring others into the secret so they could spread the word and keep the town under his spell. Rose was worried that the more people she told, the more people would be killed when they tried to go against him. She called a meeting with Martha, Geoff, Sophia, and Miles, the owner of the hardware store. Justin and Rose hoped they could be trusted to do the right thing and keep this dreadful secret to keep the other townsfolk alive.

It was seven p.m. when they all met. The figure was there, hiding in the shadows; Rose knew where to look to find him even when the others didn't.

"Right," Rose said, shaking so much that Justin held her hand to try and calm her down. "I've brought you all here tonight because you have the opportunity, the amazing opportunity, to make Friendship a perfect town. You may remember a few months ago a stranger came to our town. He'd lost his memory, so he didn't know his name or where he'd come from. Well, he's staying in town, and has made us an offer to help Friendship and rid it of anyone who doesn't contribute to making this town great. He asked me to tell several prominent people the rules, and I thought of you all. We all have family, and we all make a difference in this town. We can help the stranger, and he can help us." Rose took a deep breath before she continued. She knew this part wasn't going to be easy. "The stranger is immortal and possesses supernatural powers which will allow us to stay youthful and healthy as long as we follow his rules. We have an opportunity to keep this town we all love free from crime, poverty, and violence. He will keep us alive, as long as we do what he wants. The town and everyone living here will then prosper forever.

"What does he want in return for this good deed?" asked Miles.

Rose had dreaded this question; she knew this was going to be the hardest to answer. She took another deep breath. "He needs to feed. By feed, I mean… not food, but the people who don't contribute, who cause trouble, who don't want to get jobs or help others."

"You mean, eat people?" Miles shouted.

"He's the one that killed that couples' baby, isn't he?" Martha asked.

"Yes," said Rose, "but that was before we had an understanding, and no one has died since. But, he has a list that he's made since he's been here, watching who's not worthy of this town and the perfect existence he has in mind. You will never grow old and never die if you do as you're told."

Miles stood up. "This is disgusting. I want no part of it. I'm going to tell the police. You're all mad." Miles left, leaving Rose shaking again. She knew the figure would do something to him, but she couldn't stop it. He was too powerful.

Justin stood up next. "I think you should all sleep on it. We'll talk some more tomorrow."

Martha, Geoff, and Sophia left. Rose looked over to the corner. The figure had gone.

"He'll kill Miles, Justin," said Rose.

"I know," said Justin. "Unfortunately, that will make Martha, Sophia, and Geoff see sense and keep the secret, like us."

Rose hugged Justin. Miles was their friend, but they'd just sent him to his death; this was their fault. They knew they had no choice, though. The figure ruled the town, now.

*

Miles walked into his house and grabbed his coat. It was a long walk to the county police station; he couldn't trust Justin. He was in on it. He started along the road. It was nine p.m. by now, so it was getting dark. He thought he could hear someone behind him, but, as he turned, he saw nothing. He kept walking, mulling over what had happened in the village hall. He was so disgusted, he felt sick. All this time, Rose and Justin had known what had happened to that baby and they'd gone along with it.

Miles stopped for a breather. He shivered, suddenly feeling cold. In the distance, he could see a figure moving slowly towards him.

"Evening," he said. "It's suddenly gotten cold."

The figure stopped walking towards him and ran into the woods. Miles carried on, still thinking about the conversation in the village hall. He felt a random cold breeze again and spun around. The figure was behind him, yards away.

"What do you want?"

"You were given an opportunity tonight. You decided against it, and you are now the ammunition I need to make sure everyone else stands with Rose." The figure plunged his hand into Miles' chest and grabbed his heart. It was still beating as the figure pulled it out and started to lick the dripping blood from his hand. He bit into the heart.

"You taste good, Miles."

He loved the power he had over these humans. Normally ripping out their hearts would result in instant death, but his power could keep them conscious for a few extra precious minutes, just enough time for them to witness their final horrific demise before death finally took them.

Miles collapsed to the ground, the life draining from him. The figure leaned over him and started to drink the juices from the now dead body. He needed this feed. He'd become weak keeping Rose happy, but it was time now time to purge the unfit ones. Miles was to be the first of many. The figure took his time enjoying every bit of the juices he took; he felt his energy restoring.

He would become so powerful that no one could stop him.

13

Abigail and Sam were more determined than ever to get answers. Unfortunately, Mr. Duggee had died before he could tell them anything, so they decided to go back to the library and look through the old news reels to see if that would help. They walked into the library at about ten a.m. and decided to divide and conquer; it was going to be a long day. Abigail had left Jake with Geoff and Nipper; he'd get plenty of exercise and company there. Sam went through books of the old town dating back a hundred years, and Abigail started going through the papers. She was in her element – being a reporter, this was what she did. Abigail found an article about Jared's dad and how he was missing. Abigail didn't believe it, though – she thought it was connected to the other disappearances that had happened, and to the strange deaths. She went back further, and found a photo from 1920 of the Second Hand Rose. She looked closer and there, stood in the open door, was Rose, and behind her the wardrobe. *Wait, what?* Abigail double checked the date, and squinted at the grainy photo again – it was definitely Rose.

It was all connected – but, how? Abigail printed the information off. She was so confused; she hoped Sam was having more luck connecting the dots – Abigail just had *more* dots.

Abigail took the information over to him, and as much as the photo didn't make much sense to him either, he couldn't argue with the evidence. Disappointingly, he hadn't managed to find anything himself to provide any answers.

"Sam, we need to take this to Justin. We need to know what's happening in this town. I'll go to the shop, and I'll meet you at the sheriff's office in thirty minutes. I need to check my emails for orders – unfortunately, I still need to earn a living."

Sam and Abigail left the library and went their separate ways. Sam said he would check on Jake as he passed the bar. Abigail walked to the shop, unlocked the door, and sat behind the counter, waiting for her computer to boot up. She thought about the new information they had, and if Justin would spill the beans. She knew he was hiding something, but just wasn't sure what.

Just at that moment, she heard footsteps coming up the stairs. *Not again,* she thought. She got up and made her way to the top of the stairs, but there was a different figure there, one just as startling to see.

"Oh my God, Grandma- you're- you're dead!"

"Hello, Abigail. We need to talk. I should have explained about our protector a long time ago."

Abigail had tears rolling down her cheeks; she couldn't believe her eyes. She could barely take in what Grandma was saying. "I've missed you so much, Grandma."

"Unfortunately, we haven't got time for this. He's only given me an hour to be here, and I have a lot to tell you. Firstly, stop digging. This will end in either Jake or Sam's death. You've been warned. He respects me, so he won't take you."

Grandma went on to tell Abigail about how she met the figure, what he did for the town, and his need to feed. "It was a small price to pay," she told Abigail.

Abigail felt sick; it was too much to take in. Grandma just kept going, not even stopping to take a breath. Rose explained the figure wanted Abigail back in town, and for her to take over the shop. "He knew the only way to get you back into town was to take my life. It was important to him, because- Abigail, he..." She hesitated, and then a noise interrupted her.

"He's here," she said. "I've got to go."

Abigail saw the figure standing at the top of the stairs. She shuddered. He didn't say anything. Abigail still couldn't make out any features.

"I love you. Do as you're told, and you can't tell Sam; his life depends on it." Then, Grandma was gone.

Abigail sobbed; it was like she had said goodbye all over again.

14

Sam didn't know why he'd slept with Mary behind Abigail's back; he loved Abigail so much and he'd ruined it. When Mary became pregnant, his family had told him he had to marry her – but he didn't even love her. Living with Mary was hard. She knew he didn't love her and that he was still in love with Abigail. It had just been a stupid fling that had gotten out of hand. She got pregnant on purpose; she wanted to trap him, and it was easy. Nine months later, when Rowlf came along, Sam fell in love again. Rowlf was the most beautiful thing he'd ever seen, and he decided to try harder to make it work for Rowlf's sake. Mary never stayed home after Rowlf was born; she partied every night, leaving Sam holding the baby. Sam didn't mind, not really – he preferred Mary out of the way.

When Rowlf was two months old, Mary came home with an announcement. "Sam, I've been offered a job. It's more money, a better position, and there is even chance for me to climb the ladder. You can get a job in the local school teaching history; your job's not important anyway, you can do it anywhere."

Sam was gutted. He loved his job, and all his friends and family were in Friendship, he couldn't leave. "We'll weigh up the pros and cons," he said, trying to push the conversation his way. Mary was adamant she was leaving whether Sam wanted to go or not.

When Justin and Geoff heard Mary wanted to leave the town, they knew they had to stop her – the figure wouldn't allow it. But *how* to stop her? Geoff was on the school committee, so he recommended Sam for a promotion to the Head of History. If his job seemed more important than Mary's, then hopefully she would reconsider. It didn't work, though. Mary just laughed at Sam's news and said, "You couldn't run a department, you're useless."

Justin told Rose to talk to Sam and Mary. "They look up to you, just like everyone does in this town."

"If only I could tell them the truth, that would change their minds," she told Justin over dinner.

Sam and Mary were having breakfast one Sunday morning when they heard a knock at the door. "Hello, Rose, how are you?" Sam hugged Rose and they sat down at the kitchen table.

"Coffee?" asked Mary.

"Please."

"What brings you to our door this early, Rose?" Sam asked.

Rose hadn't slept. She'd been awake all night, thinking about what to tell Sam and Mary about why they couldn't leave, but without telling them the real reason why or what would happen if they did. "I've heard you're thinking of leaving us, Mary, for a new fancy job in the city. Well, I'm here to tell you you're too important to this town; our school needs its secretary, Mary, and our children need their history teacher. We'd fall apart if any of our important cogs leave, you understand?"

Mary nodded. "We understand, but it doesn't change anything. We're leaving. This job is too important, and it's none of your business. Goodbye, Rose."

Rose started towards the door. "This town is my business, and you've been warned. Next time, it won't be just a warning, so change your mind now before it's too late!" At that, Rose left – she knew she'd done what she could. Someone would suffer for Mary's stupidity.

*

Nothing happened for another month, other than Mary putting the house up for sale and giving in her notice at work. Mary had found an apartment for them to rent whilst they tried to sell their house in Friendship. Sam had written to other schools near to their new town for history teacher posts, but had not had any luck. He thought it was an omen not to move, but Mary just said it proved how useless he was.

About two weeks before the move, Mary was out drinking again with friends. Sam was sitting out on the veranda and Rowlf was in bed, fast asleep – Sam had just checked on him. It was a beautiful night. Sam was going to miss Friendship, but Mary had told him if he didn't go, she would stop him from seeing Rowlf ever again.

Sam heard a noise in the house. All the windows were open, as it was so warm, so he thought maybe one of the curtains had blown in the wind and knocked something over. He was too comfy to look – something he would regret for the rest of his life.

The figure entered the house. He knew Mary was out drinking and that Sam was on the back porch. He walked into Rowlf's room; there was no light on, only moonlight lit the darkness. He could hide very well in moonlight. He picked up Rowlf's blue baby blanket and wrapped Rowlf in it. He was fast asleep so didn't even murmur.

The figure took him back to the antique shop; he wanted to feed without being interrupted. Babies were his favourite delicacy. He unfolded the blanket, licking his lips. It had been years since he'd eaten something so young, so fresh. He started to feed, slowly; Rowlf woke up and started to scream.

But he didn't scream for long.

The figure crushed his skull with one hand. He didn't break his concentration, he just kept feeding, savouring every bite. An hour passed before he'd taken all Rowlf's juices, he'd enjoyed him so much.

He looked down at the shrivelled-up corpse. "Rose will tidy up later," he said. "Now your Mommy and Daddy can do anything they want. I've taught them the ultimate lesson." At that, the figure picked up the blue blanket, got back into the wardrobe, and locked the door.

15

Abigail walked into the bar. "Hello, baby boy, have you a had a lovely time with Nipper?" Jake wagged his tail; he was so happy to see Abigail.

"He's been as good as gold and better," Geoff said, patting Jake on the head.

"I need to go, Sam. I've got a lot of orders at the shop I need to pack. Come over tonight, we can talk then." Abigail clipped Jake's lead on and thanked Geoff for looking after him. "See you later, Sam. About seven p.m. – I'll cook."

Abigail left the bar, leaving Sam a little bewildered; something had clearly happened in the shop. "See you later, Geoff, thanks for the chat and pint," Sam said, making his way out.

Back in the store, Abigail boxed up the orders – she needed to keep busy. What the hell was she going to tell Sam tonight? She didn't want to leave it, but she didn't want anything to happen to either Sam or Jake; she couldn't bear that. She dropped off the parcels at the Post Office for collection in the morning and started walking home. She'd take Jake up to the mountain trail before Sam came, and, hopefully, she could clear her head and make sense of what her Grandma had told her.

Jake played in the stream whilst she sat struggling with the pros and cons of telling Sam the truth. "Argh!" she screamed. Jake turned and ran over, thinking Abigail was in pain. "Sorry, Jake, I actually feel better after that."

They walked home, and Abigail started dinner. Dead on seven p.m., there was a knock at the door. Jake barked.

"Come on in, Sam, you don't need to knock," Abigail called.

The door opened and there stood Sam, looking gorgeous. Abigail's heart skipped a beat.

"Hi, Jake. Did you have a lovely walk?" Jake wagged his tail, then ran away. He came back seconds later with his favourite toy, a cow called Daisy Moo.

"He won't give you it, Sam, he just wants you to see her," Abigail laughed. Jake was a weirdo.

"How are you, Abigail? You seemed distracted at the bar. Did something else happen in the shop?" Sam took Abigail's hand.

"We need to talk, Sam. You better open the wine and

sit down."

Abigail told Sam everything. She repeated word for word what Rose had told her. Sam looked both disgusted and shocked at the same time. Hours passed whilst both figured out what they would do with this information.

"We need to act normal, pretend we're going along with it. We need to come up with a plan to rid Friendship of this monster. Are you with me, Sam?"

Sam nodded, unable to speak; he was still taking it in. They finished making dinner but sat there looking at the food in front of them, neither of them very hungry – they just moved it around their plates. *More for Jake*, Abigail thought. He never lost his appetite. He must have thought all his Christmas's had come at once when Abigail put the chicken in his bowl.

Abigail and Sam went to bed, still mulling over what they now knew. Neither of them slept, they just tossed and turned, both devising a plan to get rid of the monster. It was five a.m. when they heard Jake bark. Abigail went downstairs to check on him and found him stood at the back door.

"Do you want to go out?" Abigail asked, opening the door to reveal a figure stood in the dark. "Justin! What are you doing here at five a.m.? What's wrong?" Abigail let Jake out and invited Justin in.

"We need to talk, Abigail. Rose didn't tell you everything; he listens in the shop, and he's tied to Rose." Justin sat down.

"Morning, Justin, where's the fire?" Sam asked as he walked into the kitchen.

"It all started in 1891." Justin started at the beginning. He asked Sam and Abigail not to interrupt him, as he had a lot to say. Abigail and Sam stared at Justin as he poured out his soul, telling them every gory detail. Abigail kept topping up the coffee – she needed it and she guessed she wasn't the only one. It was unbelievable. Abigail didn't believe a word of it, but, then again, she'd seen the figure and she'd seen Rose's ghost – it had to be true.

Justin took a breath. "We've covered up these murders for too long, it has to stop," he said, "but he's invincible. He's hundreds of years old. He takes what he needs and then moves on to the next unsuspecting town, telling them lies so he can eat children and 'the useless ones', as he puts it."

Abigail held Justin's hand. "How can we help?"

"We have to act normal," Sam said. "We have to make

sure he believes we are going along with it."

They all agreed. Justin left – he needed to go to work. "I'll see you later," he said as he shut the door.

Abigail sobbed. "If he had such a good thing going, why kill Rose?"

16

Rose and Justin were struggling with their dreadful secret; their relationship was crumbling around them. Sophia organised a party to try to cheer them both up. Rose didn't want to go but Justin talked her into it. "This is all for you, Rose," he said as they walked towards town.

Sophia greeted them both as they walked into the B-and-B. "Hi, you two, thanks for coming. Help yourself to drinks, and there's food in the kitchen."

Rose walked into the kitchen, wishing she'd never come; she wasn't in the mood for partying. She still loved Justin and she knew he loved her, but he couldn't forgive her for agreeing to the figure's demands – he was disgusted with the whole idea. Justin brought her a drink and left the kitchen to mingle. Rose decided the best way to deal with this dreadful party was to get drunk, so she downed the drink that Justin had just given her and went to get a bottle of something, because one glass at a time wasn't going to numb the pain she had. Rose downed drink after drink after drink, and Justin saw what was happening.

"You need to slow down, Rose, you're going to be ill."

Rose didn't care. She'd made up her mind to be ill; she deserved it.

It was nine p.m. They'd only been there two hours and Rose was paralytic. She couldn't stand, so Justin held on to her as she tried to walk into the kitchen.

"You need to go home, Rose. I'll take you," he said, helping her towards the door.

"I can manage, Justin. I'll get myself home. You enjoy your party, and don't bother coming home, either. We're through." Rose walked towards the door, falling into the other guests as she went. Her heart was broken.

Rose started to walk the half mile home. After only ten yards, she was violently sick as she fell into the bushes. Unable to get up, she lay there for a few minutes trying to find the strength to stand.

"Hello, you look like you need help. Can I be of assistance?"

Rose looked up and, to her surprise, before her stood the most beautiful man she'd ever seen. "Yes, thank you." Rose held out her hand, and the stranger pulled her up like she weighed nothing.

"Come on, I'll take you home."

They started to walk home, and Rose realised she wasn't drunk anymore – she was completely sober. "Who are you?" Rose asked.

"I'm a helpful stranger," the stranger giggled.

When they reached Rose's home, Rose said, "Do you want to come in for coffee?"

The stranger nodded. Rose opened the door and walked into the kitchen; the stranger followed. She could feel him close by as she turned the kettle on. The stranger reached over and turned the kettle off.

"I thought you wanted coffee," Rose said, a little confused. "Have I done something wrong? Are you leaving?"

The stranger moved towards Rose, put his hand around her waist, and kissed her. It was so passionate that Rose couldn't breathe. She kissed him back, her heart pounding. Who was this man? They made love on the kitchen floor. Rose felt like the stranger had known her all her life. He carried her upstairs to bed, and they made love again.

Rose awoke to find she was alone; the stranger had

gone. She walked downstairs, hoping he was making coffee, but no, Justin was there, asleep on the sofa. She had no idea what time he'd gotten home – she hoped it hadn't been too early and that he hadn't heard her with her mystery man.

Justin woke up. "Morning. I shouldn't have left you to walk alone last night, and I shouldn't have made you go in the first place. I think we need to talk, I'll make some coffee," he said. Rose agreed and they sat together – they were very much in love, but was it enough?

17

The summer had come and gone. It was now fall, and Sam and Abigail had seen so much of each other over the summer months. She'd had time to partly forgive him for cheating, though, she still wondered if he was in love with her or with Mary. But, right now, she was happy. Sam was normal, and, with everything else that was going on, she needed normal. They decided that having two houses was daft, as Sam spent most of his time at Abigail's anyway.

"I'll rent it out," Sam said one night over dinner. "I'll move my stuff in this weekend and ask Geoff to put a note up in the bar advertising it.

Abigail thought, *that will work out great, Jake can play with Nipper whilst we have a pint or two.* "We'll go to see Geoff Sunday afternoon." Sam knew where Abigail was going with this and was happy to go along with it.

Saturday soon came. Sam had spent all week packing box after box; he hadn't realised he had so much stuff, but it had given him the chance to throw a lot out, too, so he was glad to be doing it. He saw this as a new start with Abigail, and packing to move in with her exited him. They packed up both cars and drove to Abigail's, where Jake helped to unpack in his usual unhelpful way. It was six p.m. when they finally finished.

"Wine?" he asked. Abigail pointed to the fridge. Sam opened a bottle and poured two big glasses.

"We'll have this, then take Jake up to the mountain trail – it looks like it's going to rain." Jake loved rain, he enjoyed getting drenched. They finished their glasses and set off. It was a beautiful night, a little cooler than it had been lately, and Jake paddled whilst Sam and Abigail got to know each other a little better.

Abigail dried Jake off the best she could, and they started to walk home. They were halfway home when the heavens opened; it poured down, and Jake barked at the rain, excitedly spinning around in circles. They all ran home, not that it made any difference; they were all drenched when Abigail opened the door. She undressed in the kitchen, and Sam did the same. They grabbed some fresh clothes out of the drier and got changed before they started on the dog. Abigail grabbed Jake, but he didn't want to get dried, he was happy being wet. "Come here, bugger lugs." Jake thought she was playing, so Abigail had a fight on her hands. They were busy trying to catch him when there came a knock at the door.

"Geoff, come in. Abigail's just fighting with the wet dog. Do you want a drink?" Sam asked, watching Abigail fight with Jake behind the sofa.

"No, I'm fine, I'm not stopping, but I may have a tenant for you, someone new in town, a couple. I knew you were popping into the bar tomorrow, so I told them to come around three p.m. Is that okay?"

Sam grinned. "Thanks, Geoff, that's amazing. See you tomorrow." Geoff left, venturing back into the dreary weather. "Result!" said Sam.

"We've not met them yet, don't get ahead of yourself," Abigail laughed.

*

Sunday morning, Abigail awoke to find Sam already out of bed. She could hear him downstairs, talking to Jake.

"You'll have that dog as daft as you! Morning, Jake," she said as she entered the kitchen. Jake looked at Abigail and wagged his tail; he was always glad to see her.

"We'll take Jake out for a lovely, long walk this morning, clear the cobwebs now it's stopped raining." So, they clipped Jake's lead to his collar and off they went.

They walked for about ten miles, and Jake walked double that – he bounced all over, he had so much energy. "I think you were a duck in a past life," Abigail said, looking at Jake who was paddling again.

"Don't forget, you're seeing Nipper later, mate," Sam said.

They decided to take Jake home before going into the coffee shop for breakfast. "He can have a snooze before we go to the bar," Abigail said, thinking she'd like a snooze, too.

They walked into the coffee shop. "Morning, you two, where's Jake?" asked Jane, who looked like she was about to give birth there and then.

"He's having a snooze. We walked miles this morning, and he's got a date with Nipper later," Abigail said. "Two coffees, one sausage and one well done bacon sandwich, please, we're starving."

Sam and Abigail sat down and waited for their breakfast. "I'm happy you've moved in, and we can start over. Let's never look back, let's only look forward,"

Abigail said. She was determined she'd been given a second chance with Sam, and she wasn't going to ruin it.

"I love you, Abigail Hirst. Will you marry me?"

Abigail sat back, shocked. Where had that come from? "Yes!" she screamed.

Jane came over with breakfast. "We've just got engaged!" Abigail told her.

Jane screamed, too, which made Sam panic. "The baby!" he said, sitting Jane down.

The whole coffee shop congratulated them both. It was so amazing. Abigail thought of Rose. *She would have been so happy.* "I wish Rose was here," she said. Sam nodded.

After breakfast, Abigail decided she wanted to tell Justin and Sophia their news. Sam went back home, as he still had bits to unpack – they'd meet at Geoff's at about two-thirty p.m.

Abigail walked into the B-and-B, and announced, "We've got engaged, Sophia!"

Sophia leaped up and ran over to Abigail. "Oh my God, that's amazing news! I'm so happy for you both. I'll throw a party." Abigail remembered Sophia's infamous parties; it took days to get over them.

Abigail next went to see Justin. He was sat behind his desk when she walked in. "I have news, Justin. Sam asked me to marry him."

Justin stared at Abigail, and then a tear rolled down his cheek. "I'm so happy for you both. Have you told Sophia?"

"Yes," said Abigail. "She's going to throw us a party."

Justin knew she would. "She loves a party." Abigail said her goodbyes, and told Justin they would be at Geoff's if he had time later for a pint with them. He said, "Definitely, but I'm buying."

When Abigail walked into the bar, Sam was already there.

"Congratulations, beautiful!" shouted Geoff from the behind the bar.

"You okay?" Sam said; he thought Abigail looked strange.

"I've just told Sophia and Justin. Weird, really, Justin seemed really odd when I told him. He started to cry. I knew he thought a lot about me, but crying seemed a strange response."

"He fancies you, he clearly wanted you for himself," Sam joked.

Suddenly, Geoff shouted from behind the bar, "They're here, you two, come and meet them!"

They walked over to the bar and saw a young couple in their mid-twenties. "This is Eva and Ben, and this is Abigail and Sam. It's Sam's house that I told you about," Geoff said.

They invited the couple to sit with them and ordered some more drinks. "We'll have these, then I'll show you around," Sam said.

They made small talk. Abigail thought Ben was a little weird, but they had the money to rent Sam's house, so she could get over it. Sam took them to the house while Abigail stayed with Jake, who was playing with Nipper. It was so funny to watch; every few minutes, he checked over at Abigail to make sure she was watching, then he'd chase Nipper again.

Forty-five minutes passed, and Sam walked back into the bar. "Weird one, that Ben. I'm not sure about him, but they move in next weekend, so as long as they pay, who cares?"

18

When Abigail left town and moved to Everett, Rose asked Monica to help in the shop – she used to help in the shop with Abigail, so she knew all about the role and what to do. It was the perfect fit. One day, Rose had to go out of town to pick up a piece of furniture, so she'd left Monica on her own. She knew she could trust her, as she had been left before.

"No problem, Rose, safe journey," Monica said as Rose left. It had been a quiet day. The weather was shocking, so most people had stayed at home. Monica was bored, so she thought she'd try and get into the wardrobe that Abigail had been so obsessed with. She found a tool bag – it had a drill, a screwdriver, and a hammer inside it. "Which should I try first?" she said. "Hammer." She raised the hammer above her head and *bang*, nothing happened. She heard the doorbell and turned, but there was no one there. "Weird." When she turned back to the wardrobe, the door was open. "Even weirder." There was nothing inside. "Rose, why do you keep this ugly piece of furniture?" she said to herself as she peered inside.

"*Because I live in it.*"

Monica spun around to see a figure standing in the corner of the room. "Who are you?" she shouted.

"*Your worst nightmare. I turned a blind eye when Abigail tried to open the wardrobe, before. You won't be so lucky.*"

The figure moved towards Monica. She ran towards the stairs, but stumbled and fell down them. The figure ran after her, down the stairs to where she was lying, unable to move. He crawled on top of her; she couldn't breathe, he was so heavy. He pushed his long, gnarled, twisted fingers into her brain and felt around, feeling for the juiciest part, and he started to feed.

"*I won't kill you. Remember, you brought this on yourself.*"

She could feel the life draining out of her, but she had no fight. Monica passed out; he'd taken what he wanted. He'd left her partially brain-damaged, unable to move or talk ever again.

*

When Rose returned, the figure was waiting for her. She knew it wasn't going to be good news. Rose phoned an ambulance and Monica was taken into care. Rose blamed herself; she'd left Monica on her own. Another casualty on her conscience.

19

It was November, and the weather was turning. Abigail loved wintertime, she loved snow – not as much as Jake, though. She got excited when it snowed, as it meant Jake was happy. When Sam came home from work, he asked Abigail if she fancied a drink at Geoff's bar.

"I've had a bad day," he said, slamming about.

Abigail was never one to turn down a drink. "No problem, we'll take Jake, he can play with Nipper."

They had dinner and then walked into town; Jake knew exactly where he was going, so he pulled all the way. They entered the bar at about eight-ish. Justin and Jared were already there, and Shannon and her friends sat in one corner, giggling and gossiping.

"Hi, you three, sit down. I'll bring you some drinks over," Geoff said. "Nipper, Jake's here!" Nipper came out from behind the bar and dog-tag resumed from where they'd left off.

"Ben and Eva are here. I'll go and say hello, won't be a minute, Abigail." Sam walked over to see them. He got about halfway across the bar when Ben stood up and hit

Eva across the face. She screamed, and everyone in the bar looked up.

"Ben, what are you doing?" Sam shouted, grabbing Ben's arm as he went to hit her again.

Justin ran over and yelled, "You're coming with me, Ben."

Jared also came running over, and together they wrestled him out of the bar. As they dragged Ben out, Justin said, "You're spending the night in the cell, that will help you cool off."

Abigail shouted Jake over. "Watch him while I walk Eva home, Sam." She walked out with Eva and held out a friendly hand, which Eva grabbed thankfully. They left the bar together and walked to Sam's old house. Abigail didn't ask any questions, she was just there to make sure Eva was okay and that she got home safely.

"Coffee?" asked Eva when they reached the door.

"Love some," Abigail replied.

Eva explained that Ben had hit her for years. She'd hoped it would have stopped when they moved and got a fresh new start, but it hadn't.

"I'm here to listen, Eva, anytime you need someone." Eva nodded; she needed a friend more than anything, she didn't really have anyone.

*

Justin and Jared took Ben to the sheriff's office. "We don't have violence of any kind in Friendship, Ben. This has to stop, tonight. Sleep it off." Justin locked the door to the cell and left. As Justin walked into the office, he knew Jared wasn't the only one there. "Go home, Jared. I'll watch him. I'm sure Jane needs you more than I do." Jared left, giving a big thumbs-up as he did; Jane was about to drop, so he didn't like leaving her for too long.

"I've got this. He'll see the error of his ways, you don't need to hurt him," Justin said as the figure came into view.

"*Make sure you sort it, Justin. We don't have this behaviour in Friendship.*" The figure left.

Justin sighed. He needed to put a lid on this.

*

As Sam and Abigail walked home, they talked about their interesting night and poor Eva. Abigail knew the figure would strike if Ben hit her again, and maybe that was the best outcome in the long run.

Winter came and went, and Abigail and Eva became really good friends, spending much of their time together over the next few months. Abigail never talked about Ben hitting Eva, but she saw the bruises, so she knew it hadn't stopped. She just hoped Eva would get strong enough to ask him to leave. Either way, she was there for her when she needed to talk.

"See you tomorrow, Eva," Abigail said as she hugged Eva goodbye.

"Thank you, Abigail, for another amazing day. Enjoy your Sunday." They parted ways. Abigail hoped she wouldn't get home to an angry Ben.

The next morning when Abigail awoke, she could smell breakfast cooking. "I'm starving!" she shouted.

"You better get down here, then!" Sam shouted back, and Jake followed that with a bark.

They had breakfast, then decided Sam would take Jake for a walk into the mountains and Abigail would go to the shop. She had emails to reply to and Sunday was the best day for that; no customers, just peace and quiet. She loved work, but she loved walking Jake more – she would take him again later, he'd be happy with two mountain walks.

Abigail said goodbye to her boys and headed into town, saying hello to everyone who was out and about that gorgeous morning. She opened the shop, and a cold shudder went down her spine. "You're here, aren't you?" She could see the figure at the back of the shop.

"I won't hurt you; we need to talk about Ben."

Abigail walked towards the figure. For the first time, she could make out what he looked like. He was thin, and his skin seemed to hang away from his bones. When he realised Abigail was able to see him clearly, he backed off into the shadows. Abigail told him she would speak to Ben and tell him he couldn't stay if he was going to hit Eva. The figure seemed happy.

"I'll leave it to you, but you only get one try." At this, he left, and Abigail caught her breath.

"Work, Abigail, that will take your mind off the figure and death."

It was about one p.m. when Abigail looked at the clock. "Lunch!" She walked towards the door and was just about to lock it when it swung open. There stood Eva with blood running down her head.

"He's worse than ever, it's as though this town brings out the worst in him," she sobbed.

Abigail brought her in, sat her down, and started to clean the wound. Eva was shaking; she knew Ben would never stop. She kept looking at the door, clearly scared he would show up at any moment. Abigail knew the figure was there, watching the whole thing, so she knew she couldn't tell Eva what was about to happen. Maybe she could get Ben to leave, and that would sort it out.

Out of the corner of her eye, she saw the figure go down into the basement.

"I just need to get something from the basement, Eva, stay here," she said before heading down the stairs.

"*He's mine, now,*" the figure said.

"No, let me talk to Ben," Abigail whispered. "I'll get him to leave, give me one chance to save him." The figure nodded his agreement.

Abigail called Sam and asked him to sit with Eva while she talked Ben into leaving. He was at the shop about twenty minutes later with Jake. Seeing Sam and Jake seemed to calm Eva down. Sam, though, was quietly worried; if Ben could hit Eva, who he loved, then what would he do to Abigail, who he didn't even know?

"I won't be long," Abigail assured them, then left the shop and walked to Sam's old house.

*

Ben answered the door and stared at her. "Hi, Ben, can I come in? I think we need to talk." Ben wasn't listening – this was going to be hard. "Friendship is the perfect town, don't you think? We all think so, and there is a reason it's perfect; it's because we don't have any bad elements. No fighting. It's like one big, happy family."

Just then, Ben lunged at her, punching her in the face. Abigail hit the ground, hard.

"Shut up, witch!"

Ben hit her again, this time in the back. Abigail crawled into the house; she knew where the phone was, and she'd left hers in the shop. Ben followed her.

"Where are you going, witch?" Ben hit her again. Abigail screamed, hoping someone would hear her.

Someone heard, alright. He was there, and he was going to save her. Ben would regret ever laying a hand on Eva, and especially on Abigail. The figure was hungry, and he was going to enjoy this.

Abigail, at this point, was struggling to stay conscious, which was a godsend with what was about to happen – at least this death wouldn't stay on her conscience. The figure punched Ben to the ground. He'd never killed in broad daylight before – this was new. He reached into Ben's chest, slowly squeezing his lungs. Ben tried to fight, but the figure ripped off both of his arms, throwing them away like dolls' arms. He pulled out his hand and plunged it in again, this time grabbing his heart. He squeezed, harder this time, making Ben yell out. The figure ripped out his tongue. He wanted quiet. He wanted to savour this moment. He pulled out Ben's liver – he hadn't eaten liver for decades. He bit into it while Ben watched in horror.

"This is what happens to people like you. I will kill you while you watch."

The figure licked the blood from his hands, then pulled off one of Ben's legs. He tore off the flesh with his teeth, like he was eating ribs. Licking his lips, he went for the other leg. Ben was trying to get away, pushing himself with his leg to the door. The figure grabbed and pulled the other leg off, then smashed it down on Ben's head, crushing his skull.

It was a shame these pathetic humans succumb to death so quickly. At least he had the extra few minutes his powers allowed to prolong their pain and anguish longer, for his pleasure.

The figure took his time as he finished devouring Ben. He kept one eye on Abigail the whole time, making sure she didn't wake; he didn't want her to see him, to see what he was.

"Abigail, are you alright?"

Abigail awoke to Justin and Geoff standing over her.

"I'm okay… What happened?" Abigail started to look around the room, hunting for Ben.

"We chased Ben out of town. He's gone, thankfully," Geoff said, helping Abigail to her feet.

The sheriff and Geoff took Abigail to the shop, where Sam and Eva where waiting.

"Oh my God, Abigail, are you okay?" Eva came over to help Justin and Geoff sit Abigail down.

"She's fine, just a little shaken. Ben has gone. He's left town. You'll see no more of him, Eva. No more beatings. He's out of your life, period." Justin nodded at Geoff and they both left.

Sam was hugging Abigail like he'd not seen her in

years. Jake, on the other hand, was licking Abigail's hand; she had a cut, and he was making it better, so he thought.

Abigail was numb. She couldn't feel the cuts and bruises all over her body. "I want to go home. You can stay at our house, Eva. Maybe you shouldn't be alone tonight."

Eva nodded. She didn't want to go home just yet; the company was what she needed. They all walked home in silence until they reached the house.

"I'll walk Jake, Abigail, while you sort Eva. Is that okay?" Abigail assured Jake she was fine, and he went with Sam.

20

Michael and Christian were cleaners. Not in the usual way – dusting and hoovering – but in the way of cleaning towns of useless people, the people who didn't make a difference or contribute in any way. They'd done this job for centuries, and they were the best. They would offer the town's more prominent residents immortality, and in return they would turn a blind eye to the horrors. It was the perfect deal – unless, of course, you fell into the wrong category. The townsfolk were too scared to confront Michael and Christian once they'd seen what they could do, so the demons had the run of the town, taking the lives of people who either crossed them or that they didn't like the look of.

Unfortunately, Michael got cocky. He started to take babies in the night. They were his favourites, his weakness. Christian warned him it would be his undoing, but Michael couldn't resist – he kept taking. Whenever he had the itch, he'd scratch it.

It was easier back in the Fourteenth Century. People didn't fight back as much, especially in those glorious plague infested years. But, as the centuries rolled on, people became more and more wary of strangers, so they both had to get inventive. Michael would tell the townsfolk he was an angel sent from God to do God's work, and if they didn't obey, God would take their children – this way, they never suspected he had eaten them. This worked for a while, until Michael was caught eating a two month old and the pitch forks came out. Michael killed the whole town, and after that he changed his tact.

Michael and Christian began life as humans, but they were both killers, both evil men. When their crimes were brought to the town's attention, they were both hung and condemned to hell. They never actually made it to Hell, however; they were left in Purgatory, whereon meeting a demon they were given a second chance to use their skills for a different purpose, a useful purpose. This suited them both, and, to get out of Purgatory, they accepted the job.

*

It was 1852 when Michael was sent to a town which badly needed cleansing. The town had an orphanage which was run by a lady who was renowned for her beauty. Her husband was much older than her, and he always feared she would eventually stray. Unfortunately for him, she did.

One night, whilst working late, the woman and a male companion had a little too much to drink – the woman had lured him there, and he was quite willing. They made love on the office floor, table, and pretty much anywhere that could hold them. The next day, when Michael found out, he warned her that it mustn't happen again, but she ignored him and did the same the very next night.

Michael was enraged. He pulled the front door of the orphanage clean off its hinges. The woman screamed, but Michael pushed her aside; he was determined she was going to watch everything that was about to happen. This was all her fault. Michael ripped her lover in half, throwing the two parts across the room. He then dragged her upstairs to the children's rooms. He broke down the doors, making the children scream and run about. The first child he caught, he tore off his legs and ripped the flesh from his bones. Michael had lost control; he was having so much fun. A little girl, about five, was hiding under her bed. Michael lifted it and grabbed her, pulling her up by her leg and biting into her head, sending blood up the walls. Child after child died that night in similarly gruesome ways. There were bits of them all over the orphanage. Michael was so full by now that he was just killing for fun, just for the hell of it.

When all the children were dead, he walked up to the woman and laughed. He'd made his point.

Michael left. He never looked back, just moved on to the next town. The woman killed herself shortly after; she couldn't live with what she had done. This was her fault, and no one would believe her, anyway.

When Christian heard what Michael had done, he vowed never to feed on humans from thereon, and to follow Michael and prevent him from ever going too far again. He vowed that if Michael crossed the line, he would stop him for good.

21

Abigail told Sam and Eva everything when he and Jake came back. Eva didn't believe it at first, but then it all started to make sense – Ben was a bully, but he wouldn't have left her unless something had happened to him. Eva knew he was dead; it was the only explanation that made any sense. They all decided it was now time, time to take the town back from this monster before anyone else died.

"How do we do it?" Sam said, hoping Abigail would have all the answers.

"No idea," she said, hoping something would hit her out of the blue.

They all went to bed. "Maybe the answer will come to us in the night," Abigail hoped.

Something would come, but it wasn't answers.

Abigail woke up to a noise downstairs and Jake growling. "What is it, what can you hear?" Abigail asked him as she got out of bed and started to walk downstairs. She left Jake in the bedroom, because deep down she knew what was downstairs and she couldn't risk Jake getting hurt.

"*Abigail, I won't hurt you. I just wanted to make sure you were safe,*" a voice came from downstairs.

"What did you do to Ben?"

"*Ben's dead. He won't hurt anyone else. This town will stay perfect, and no one will jeopardise that. NO ONE!*" The figure disappeared.

Abigail ran back upstairs. Jake was now barking. Sam shouted her name and ran out of the bedroom to meet her.

"He's just been here – we need to destroy him!" Abigail shouted as Eva opened the bedroom door. "Time for a plan."

They sat up all night, trying to figure out how to get rid of him. It was six a.m. when Abigail said, "A fire! We need to burn down the Second Hand Rose and, more importantly, burn that damn wardrobe."

"That's it, Abigail! You're a genius," Sam said, kissing Abigail. "We need to act normal, make sure he doesn't suspect anything."

Eva agreed. "We need him to think we're all going along with it and catch him off guard."

The plan was in motion. They all sat at the breakfast table, working out their part of this monster's downfall. They all had very important parts to play, and it needed to be perfect; no mistakes. No one else could know.

"Coffee, anyone? It is morning, after all," Abigail asked as they settled their plans.

They all got showered and dressed to go to work. Abigail and Eva went to the shop. They decided they would never talk of their plan, just in case he was listening; they couldn't risk it. Sam went to his class, but his mind wasn't on schoolwork, he had so much going through his head. The day seemed to drag, minutes felt like hours, and the day couldn't end quickly enough. Abigail had told Sam to meet them after work in the bar – she wanted to act as normal as possible, and the bar was as good a place to start.

"Hi, Abigail, how are you?" Geoff patted Jake on the head – he had to be quick, Jake had seen Nipper, so the inevitable dog tag was on again. Abigail laughed as Jake and Nipper ran all over the pub, just missing the people sat at the bar. "He's a character, Abigail. Sit over there, I'll bring your drinks. Is Sam joining you both?"

"He should be here any minute." Right then, Sam walked through the door. Jake ran over to say hi, then he was off again chasing Nipper, barking every few minutes when Nipper caught him. Abigail started rummaging around in her bag and realised she had left Jake's treats in the shop, and he would not be happy with that.

"Sorry, Sam, I've forgotten something at the shop. Stay with Jake and Eva, I won't be long."

Abigail walked across the road and opened the door to the shop. As she did so, a cold shiver went down her spine.

"*Come here. You need to understand you can't beat me.*"

Abigail reluctantly walked to the back of the shop where she could she the figure stood.

"*I won't hurt you; you mean too much to me. You know who I am, now. I'm here to help. But what keeps me here is you. I could have moved on a long time ago, but then Rose became pregnant. With you.*"

Abigail didn't understand. Rose wasn't her mother, she was her grandmother. Her parents had died when she was three months old in a fire, and Rose had taken her in. "You lie! You say I mean something to you, and then you lie!" Abigail shouted.

"*I never lie. I have no reason to. You are Rose's daughter. She had to say your parents had died, she looked too old to be your mother. Did you not think it peculiar there are no photos of your parents before the supposed fire, and no photos of Rose before you were born? You are the spitting image of your mother, of Rose. You must see it."*

Abigail thought he must be right. There were no photos of her parents. Rose had told her they had all gone up in the fire, but why didn't Rose have some in her house?

"I loved Rose, she's why I chose this town. I was passing through; I was weak and needed a place to recover. Rose patched me up, so I stayed. Rose couldn't have children, she and Justin tried for so long, but it wasn't meant to be. So, I gave her what she wanted. ABIGAIL, I AM YOUR FATHER!"

Abigail passed out cold on the floor.

*

Abigail woke up. Looking at the clock, it had only been moments since she'd fallen down, but the figure was gone. She was shaking with fear, and feeling so sick at the same time. Pushing through the sickness, she pulled herself up and walked to the sheriff's office; there was something she needed to say.

She barged into the building. "You didn't tell me everything, Justin. Rose is my mother, and the monster is my father. How could you keep that from me? He's just told me everything."

Justin stopped her. "I am your father, not that monster. I don't understand why he would say he's your father."

Abigail was too upset to listen. She turned, walked out of the sheriff's office, and went straight home. She needed time on her own. One thing she did know: the monster needed to die. He'd ruined too many lives. It had to stop now. The recent revelation made it even more imperative.

22

Justin was so upset about what Abigail had said the day before that he decided he would confront the figure; he needed to know why he would tell Abigail he was her father. He walked over to the shop, stopped for a moment to gather his thoughts, then unlocked the door and walked in.

"Where are you, you monster? Come out and face me!" Justin shouted. "Coward! Where are you?"

"Watch it, Justin," a voice came from the back of the shop. He was here. Justin shuddered. *"What do you want?"* the figure asked.

"Why would you tell Abigail you're her father? Rose would have never slept with you, you're disgusting!"

"She did have sex with me, and I gave her Abigail because you were inadequate. You couldn't give her a child." Suddenly, the figure transformed into a gorgeous man. *"This was the person Rose had sex with, and she couldn't get enough. She obviously needed me."*

The figure was angry, Justin could tell, but Justin was angry, too. He'd believed he was Abigail's father. Rose had never told him about sleeping with this thing.

"*You worthless piece of trash. You think you can come against me and win? What did you think would happen when you came over here?*"

The figure came closer. Justin had only ever seen him properly three times before. "You need to leave this town alone. Rose is dead, now. We don't need you anymore!" Justin shouted, then moved back towards the door.

"*Really, Justin, where do you think you're going?*" The figure ran towards Justin, grabbing him by the throat and pulling him further into the shop. Justin tried to yell, but his voice didn't come out; the figure's hand was so tightly gripped. The figure dragged Justin into the basement. "*Privacy, Justin. I like privacy when I eat. Don't be surprised; the town has new blood, now, and my daughter's back here at last. There are new people to rule. I don't need you, Geoff, or Sophia. You're all redundant.*"

The figure stopped and loosened his grip. Justin swallowed; he knew what was going to happen. He didn't fight or even try to escape. He'd been alive for over a hundred years and was tired of doing what the figure asked, sick of being ruled.

The figure started to back away. Justin was confused, what was he doing? Then, he rushed forwards, pushing his hands into Justin's chest. Justin screamed. The figure pulled out his ribs, ripping them clean out of his chest. The figure first licked up the blood, then ate the flesh. Justin stood, unable to move as he watched the figure eat.

"Nice, Justin, you've matured well," the figure said, licking his lips.

Once the figure had eaten all the flesh off the ribs, he looked straight at Justin. Justin knew he was about to die, but it was up to the figure whether it was a quick death or not. He started to smell Justin around his head and hair. Justin took a deep breath.

"I won't make you suffer."

He ripped Justin's head clean off his shoulders. Justin's limp body fell to the floor. The figure pulled out his brain and swallowed it in one. Then, he drank Justin's body, stopping halfway through to savour the glorious taste. He knew Rose would not be happy, but Justin had known the consequences for confronting him.

"They never learn, Rose. Never!"

23

It was 1348 when Michael and Christian arrived in London. The plague was in full throw and thousands were dying – no one would notice a few more bodies. Michael and Christian would be able to feed, and no one would question it. Bodies were everywhere, the streets had piles of them. Rats were running all over the corpses whilst crows happily pecked out the juicy eyeballs. Michael and Christian didn't like the taste of the plague-ridden bodies, – the juices were sour – so they had to kill people who hadn't been touched by the plague. Michael took babies, and, by the time he'd finished with them, they looked like the plague had taken them, all shrivelled up and disfigured. Christian liked young women, untouched by man, pure. Both had the time of their lives; it was play-time with no consequences.

Michael found a child at home, alone. He checked its mother wasn't close by before he entered the house, heart racing. He loved the kill. He licked his lips; he could taste the child already. Leaning over the cot, Michael sank his teeth into the child's head, spraying the room with blood.

This child was plague free – he always checked. He had made a mistake earlier in the week and it was disgusting, like drinking spoiled milk. The child was semi-conscious, no crying. He hated crying. It brought onlookers. He plunged his hand into the child's chest and pulled out its heart. It kept beating with shallow beats, in shock from being pulled out. But it stopped as Michael bit into it. He closed his eyes in delight.

Then out of the calm came a scream: "My baby! You monster!"

The scream was short lived, as Christian came up behind her and plunged his hand into her chest, ripping her heart out, smashing her ribs. He was stronger than Michael and always had been. "Waste not, want not." Christian fed on her heart, licking the blood from his arm. "We must go," he said, "before we have more company."

They left the bodies where they were. It had been a feast, and they now needed somewhere to sleep, to gather their strength back. Michael found a sewerage tunnel near the River Thames – it wasn't ideal, but no one would look in there. It was disgusting, but it meant they could sleep undisturbed.

*

When they awoke, it was early morning. "I'm starving, time for breakfast," Michael said, turning to Christian.

"Baby, child, or something different?" Christian was hungry, too.

They crawled out of the tunnel, making sure no one spotted them, and walked into town.

"Christian, look." Michael had spotted twin girls, maybe early teens.

Christian stopped, turned to Michael. "I think we've just found breakfast."

They followed the girls, hoping they would turn up an alley or go to a quieter part of the city. When they started to walk between the houses, Michael and Christian got ready – their hearts were racing, and they were starting to sweat.

They sprung. It was quiet in the alley, and Michael and Christian took their time; they were not going to be rushed. Michael started with the girl's head and Christian with the other girl's legs, each enjoying every bite, every juicy bite; there was blood everywhere. They couldn't decide whether to lick the blood up or take the next bite.

The feed took hours. When done, Michael sat back. He'd had so much fun and so much food he was going to burst. Christian looked at Michael. "They were beautiful, best breakfast ever." Michael agreed.

24

Abigail spent all day looking for Justin. She asked Geoff, Sophia, and Jared if anyone had seen him since yesterday. Abigail walked around town until she couldn't walk any more. Jake stood, looking up at her. "I think Justin's dead, Jake," she said, finally admitting what she'd suspected in her head for the last two hours. "Oh my God, he's killed him." She sat down in front of the shop, unable to go inside.

At that moment, Sam walked up to her. "Abigail, what's wrong?" he said, stroking Jake.

"Nothing, Sam, sorry. Just walked Jake, he wanted ten miles today, he's never tired." Abigail didn't want the figure to hear her, she knew he was listening. "Home, I think, you two." Abigail stood up and passed Jake's lead to Sam. As they walked home together, Sam tried to make conversation, but Abigail wasn't really listening; she had too much on her mind. She needed to tell Sam that Justin was dead and that their plan to rid Friendship of the figure had to be brought forward. As soon as they walked through the door, Abigail blurted it all out.

Sam stood stiff as a board, holding his breath until

Abigail finished, then he gasped for air. "Abigail, oh my God, are you sure?" Sam didn't want to believe it, but he knew it was true. He hated the figure, he wanted to kill him, but he was still unsure how to do it.

"Where's Jake?" Abigail suddenly looked around, but he wasn't in the kitchen or living room.

"Jake! Where are you, puppy dog?" Sam started running about, shouting Jake. Nothing.

*

Unbeknownst to Abigail and Sam, Jake had gotten out of the house and was walking into town; he knew the way, he'd done it a hundred times before, but this time he was on a mission. This time, it was time to finally sort out the figure, once and for all.

He went around the back of the shop; he knew Abigail didn't dead bolt the door, so he could easily push it open. He walked inside, and could feel the figure watching.

"*Hello, Christian,*" the figure said as Jake turned back into Christian, Michael's old friend.

"Hello, Michael, looks like you're up to your old tricks. Where's Justin? I'm guessing he's dead. You need to move on, now, or I will contact Purgatory and ask them to take you back. I'm Abigail's protector, and I won't let you hurt anyone else in this town. MOVE ON, MICHAEL! Before this gets any worse," Christian warned.

"I'm having fun, Christian. You remember fun, don't you? Or do you just kill rats, now? How long has it been since you've killed a human, a baby?"

Christian shuddered. He didn't kill anymore, not since 1852 when Michael killed all those children in the orphanage. "I'm stronger than you, Michael. This is your only warning."

Suddenly, they heard the door open. "Jake? Where are you?" Abigail shouted.

Christian turned back into Jake and barked as he ran upstairs towards Abigail, who started to cry the moment she saw him. "Thank God, I was worried! How did you get back here?"

25

Abigail and Sam walked back to the house in silence. Sam was wondering why Jake would go back to the shop on his own; what had possessed him? When they arrived home, Abigail started to make dinner and fed Jake. "You silly dog, don't do that again," she said as she put his bowl down.

Sam decided he would go into town tomorrow – it would be a Sunday. He would find out why Jake went to the shop. He didn't mention it to Abigail, though.

After dinner, they sat on the veranda with a glass of wine. "Are you okay, Abigail?" Sam asked. She was awfully quiet, and he was worried.

"I couldn't bear it if anything happened to Jake or you, you're my world. We need to just carry on with our lives and forget fighting the figure, it's not worth killing ourselves over it. We'll never win. He's too powerful."

Sam kept quiet. He knew in the morning he was going to do the very opposite. They both sat enjoying the warm night, laughing as they watched Jake chase bugs.

"You daft dog," Abigail said as he caught a wasp,

which then stung him on his mouth.

They went to bed at midnight. "We'll take Jake for a long walk tomorrow, Sam," Abigail said as she got into bed.

"I have few errands in the morning, so you take him, and I'll see you later on," Sam said, hoping Abigail wouldn't ask questions.

*

Abigail had already taken Jake out when Sam got up – she'd left a note saying she'd see him later, planning to have lunch in the pub around one p.m. Sam hoped he'd make it, he feared what would happen when he got to the shop; he'd not seen the figure and he wasn't sure what he was capable of.

He started the walk into town, then changed his mind and started to walk back, only to turn around again. He paused, not sure if had the courage to go through with his plan. "Maybe this isn't a good idea," he said to himself, but he plucked up the courage to start again.

He arrived at the shop, unlocked the door, walked in, and shut the door behind him, deciding not to lock it just in case he needed to make a quick getaway. He moved towards the wardrobe and banged on the doors. "Where are you? It's time we talked!" he shouted.

Sam suddenly felt cold and shuddered; the figure was there.

"What do you want, Sam? Why have you come here?"

"No one wants you here. You're killing people for fun, that's not what you're supposed to do. You're only supposed to kill the bad people in town, which is still disgusting, but that's what Rose and the others signed up for."

"I'll do whatever I want, Sam. Do you think you can stop me? I don't think so."

Sam took a deep breath. "You'll change your mind, you'll see." Sam turned towards the door, but the figure grabbed him and pulled him back into the shop.

"I don't think so, Sam. No one threatens me."

The figure put his hands around Sam's throat – Sam tried to scream, but nothing came out. He threw Sam to the floor, sitting on top of him, squeezing his chest. Sam couldn't breathe.

The figure laughed. *"You're not good enough for my daughter, you're not even a man."* As the figure applied more pressure to his chest, Sam heard his ribs crack. The pain was excruciating, and he couldn't draw a breath. Everything was starting to go dark, and his consciousness started to slip away.

"*You don't get away that easy,*" the figure said, as he made sure Sam was fully conscious again.

Suddenly, the door opened, and in walked Jake. He changed into Christian, and pulled Michael off Sam, throwing him across the room. Sam passed out cold. Christian and Michael started to fight one another. Christian was enraged. He ripped off Michael's right arm, hitting him with it. Michael knew he wasn't going to win, so he retreated into the safety of the wardrobe. Christian turned back into Jake, and ran into the street, barking as loud as he could. Geoff was walking by and heard Jake, followed him back into the shop, and came to Sam's rescue.

26

Sam was taken straight into hospital; he was struggling to breathe and was clearly in a lot of pain. Abigail asked Geoff to look after Jake and got into her car to follow the ambulance. When she arrived at the hospital, she asked the receptionist where Sam had been taken and was directed to the door at the end of the corridor which said 'Surgery Waiting Room'. Abigail started to cry as the realisation of what had happened finally sunk in.

Hours passed. She saw nurses coming and going past the windows of the door, but no one came in with any news. Abigail sat there, trying to keep her mind off the worst. She knew it was the figure who had done this, but why did he spare him? Why didn't he kill Sam, and why was Jake there?

Finally, a doctor came into the waiting room. "Miss Hirst?" he said. "Sam's doing well, but he's cracked six ribs and punctured a lung, so we've put him on a ventilator, which looks a lot worse than it is. Don't panic when you see him, he's lost a lot of blood, so we've given him a transfusion."

Abigail followed the doctor into Recovery and there lay Sam, all hooked up to heart monitors and machines to check his breathing. She stopped and took a deep breath.

"Hi, Sam, I'm here," said Abigail. She sat down beside his bed. "Jake's fine, Geoff has him, looks like he saved your life, he'll expect lots of biscuits when we get home."

Abigail fell asleep in the bed beside Sam's – a nurse came in to wake her. "Go home, Miss Hirst, you need to rest," she said.

Abigail drove home, still shaking. She stopped at Geoff's to pick up Jake who was so happy to see her, he cried with joy.

Abigail didn't sleep at all. She tossed and turned, going over what had happened to Sam. It was seven a.m. when she finally decided to get up, and she called the hospital as soon as she walked into the kitchen. "He's doing really well, Miss Hirst, you take your time coming in," the nurse said on the other end of the phone.

She walked Jake, mostly because she'd missed him, but also to clear her head; it was going to be a long day. Geoff had told her that Jake could stay with him if she needed. It was ten a.m. when she dropped Jake off with

Geoff. "Give him our love, Abigail. If you need anything, please just ask," Geoff said.

"Okay, Geoff, thanks again. I'll call back later to update you, but the hospital is happy with his progress so far."

When Abigail arrived at the hospital, it dawned on her: she'd been back in Friendship exactly one year. *And what a year*, she thought. The doctor was in Sam's room when she got there.

"He's doing well, Miss Hirst. We're pleased with his responses. He's had a really good night and he's trying to breathe on his own. He's a fighter." The doctor left, and Abigail sat beside Sam and started to read. She'd been wanting to read this book for five years, so this seemed like a good time to finally start it.

*

Over the next six weeks, Sam got stronger and stronger, and when Abigail walked in one Sunday morning, he was awake.

She screamed, "Oh my god, Sam! How are you doing?"

"I'm alive, no thanks to the figure; he tried to kill me. How's Jake?" he said.

"Trust you to think of Jake. He's really good. Missing you, though."

The doctor came in to check on Sam. "Morning, you two," he said. "Told you he was a fighter. Keep this up, and you'll be home in another four weeks."

Abigail left the room while the doctor examined him. She called Geoff with the good news. "Can you tell Sophia and Eva, please, Geoff? They'll be so happy he's awake."

*

The doctor was right. Sam got stronger and stronger, and, after four weeks, like promised, Sam came home. Jake bounced on him when he walked through the door.

"Jake, be gentle, Daddy's still poorly," Abigail said as Jake whizzed around the room.

Sam slept for two days solid – being in his own bed, and the fact there were no nurses poking him, helped. Abigail and Jake kept out of his way and let him sleep; she kept looking in on him every hour or so just in case he'd woken up.

Eventually, Abigail heard footsteps coming down the stairs. "Morning, you two," Sam said as he entered the kitchen.

"How ya doing? Are you hungry?" Abigail asked.

"Starving. I'm so hungry, I could eat Jake's food!" Sam winked at Jake.

27

One September morning, Sam, who was now nearly fully recovered, decided some fresh air was needed. He grabbed Jake's lead, at which point Jake went berserk.

"Calm down, nutter, we're definitely going." Sam clipped on the lead and off they went.

Abigail hadn't left Sam alone for long periods until today, so this was the first time he'd been alone with Jake – the first time he could find out who Jake really was. He knew there was something going on. They walked up the track to the stream, Sam unclipped the lead, and Jake went paddling.

"Right, Jake," Sam said. "What the hell are you?"

Jake turned. He hung his head; he knew the game was up. Jake turned into a man right in front of Sam, and Sam fell over onto his backside. "My name is Christian."

"Oh my God, I didn't dream it! You *are* human!" Sam gasped; he couldn't believe his eyes.

"I'm not human, Sam. I think you'd better stay sat down and get comfortable; I've got a lot to tell you."

Christian told Sam everything. He left nothing out, not

even the gory details; he had nothing to lose. Now Sam knew, he would probably tell Abigail – the game was over, so he may as well tell the whole truth. Sam went white at some of the stories, but Christian just kept going. He wanted Sam to know everything so he couldn't later say: "You didn't tell me that!"

"Why did you become a dog, Jake? Christian – sorry, it's a lot to take in," Sam asked when Christian finished his story.

"I heard Abigail talking to someone in the bar in her old town. She said she'd love a dog, and that the right dog would just find her. So, I turned into a dog and found her. She's my best friend, and Michael will not have her; she's his daughter, and he thinks he can pass the family business onto her. It's not happening, Sam, and we'd better stop him. Are you with me, or are you going to tell Abigail everything?"

Sam promised he wouldn't tell anyone about Christian's secret – at least for now. Plus, he knew no one would believe him anyway, he'd probably just get locked up. They walked back to the house where Abigail was waiting. She'd started dinner.

"How's my favorite boys? Have you two been

behaving?" Abigail said, hugging Sam and reaching a hand out for Jake to shove his wet nose into.

After dinner, Jake curled up in his bed, snoring and kicking out his back leg every now and again, and letting out the occasional bark. "He's dreaming about his walk with you, Sam. He must have had a great time. I'm glad you're friends, I do love him so much," Abigail said as she squeezed Sam's hand.

"He's a tough little devil, Abigail. He saved my life, as far as I'm concerned. He's an angel and deserves a medal." Sam squeezed Abigail's hand back.

Jake – who had woken up slightly – looked at Sam and winked. He knew Sam would help him get rid of Michael for good. The question was how.

28

Jake walked into town. He was determined Michael would leave Friendship – he would give him no choice. It was now or never. This had gotten out of hand, but this time he was going to put a stop to it for good. He entered the shop. "Where are you, Michael? We need to talk!" Jake shouted as he transformed into Christian.

Michael appeared out of the wardrobe. *"Hello, my old friend, I've been expecting you."*

"You must leave, Michael, this is your last warning. This town doesn't need you anymore. You'd better go before you or someone else gets hurt."

Michael laughed; he could tell Christian meant business, but he was having too much fun to leave.

Christian had plans, and none of them involved Michael; it had to stop, the killings had to stop. Christian lunged at Michael pushing him to the ground – his arm had partly grown back from their last fight. They smashed each other to the ground, neither of them noticing the oil lanterns that fell as they threw each other about. Punching each other in the face and stomach, they fell against the furniture in the shop, knocking over the Tiffany lamps which smashed and crackled as the electric cables came away from the bases. One sparked as it hit the floor, but Michael and Christian didn't notice the oil or the sparks – they were too busy hitting each other. Blood flew across the shop, hitting the ceiling and floor as Michael fell against a sideboard, the force of his fall pushing it over and causing the mirror on top to smash against the floor. Michael managed to overpower Christian, pushing him to the ground, and another Tiffany lamp crashed to the floor. Christian reached out a hand, feeling around for something to hit Michael with. He grabbed a piece of the broken mirror and plunged it into Michael's chest, tearing at his flesh. Michael fell back, hitting the wardrobe with his full force. Christian pulled out the piece of mirror and plunged it in again. Michael yelled as he pulled the shard of glass out of this chest, and he stumbled forward, slipping in the oil. In the background, one of the torn electric cables sparked, causing the oil to ignite. Christian could see what was about to happen as Michael was desperately trying to stand, blood pouring from his chest. Suddenly, there was an explosion. One of the gas canisters Abigail had for the heating caught fire, throwing them both across the room.

Christian saw his chance; he picked up the piece of mirror and plunged it again into Michael's chest, but he managed to get free from Christian's grasp. He pulled open the wardrobe door and climbed in, thinking he would be safe, safe from Christian's brute strength. Christian shut the door and jammed it shut, exactly at the same time as the second gas canister exploded, engulfing the whole shop.

*

At the same time the fight was starting, Abigail and Sam were on their way to the shop, looking for Jake, and bumped into Geoff and Sophia who were stood outside, near the store. They could hear the commotion inside, and could smell the burning of the fire and oil.

"Have you seen Jake?" Abigail asked Geoff with panic in her voice.

"I think he went in there, Abigail, but I don't know what he can do – he's just a dog."

Abigail screamed Jake's name and started running towards the shop as the explosion happened. She was floored with the force of the blast but was far enough away to not be too badly hurt. They all rushed to check on Abigail who was now sobbing on the ground, knowing she had lost Jake.

At that exact moment, right in front of Sam and Abigail, both Geoff and Sophia started to age quickly. It reminded Abigail of the *Indiana Jones* movie when the bad guy drank from the incorrect 'Cup of Christ'. They didn't seem to be in pain – almost relieved would be the best way to describe them, as if years of guilt and burden had somehow been lifted from them in an instant. As Abigail and Sam watched on in horror, they turned to dust.

Abigail turned to Sam and said, "It's finally over, Sam, the figure must be dead. But at what cost?"

Suddenly, out of the smoke, they saw movement; a small figure crawled out of the rubble. Abigail looked up to see Jake hobbling out of the door, which was now the only thing left standing of the whole shop. He was black with smoke, and he was clearly in pain as he limped towards them.

Abigail screamed, "Jake, you're alive! Oh my god, how are you, are you okay?" She picked him up. He was covered in blood and had glass in his paw. "We'll make you better than brand new, puppy boy."

Jake was fine. He and Sam knew what had happened. Jake – or, Christian – had saved Friendship, and, more importantly, saved Abigail.

*

Three months passed. Abigail and Sam adopted Nipper and took over the bar; Eva took over the B-and-B, and, unfortunately, all those cats. Sam did, in the end, keep his promise to Christian, and Abigail was blissfully unaware of who Jake really was. And that was how it was meant to be. Life was pretty amazing, and Abigail could finally enjoy that glass of wine, sat on the veranda with Jake and Sam.

THE END?

Epilogue

Two years later.

Across the world, in a chocolate box village in Sweden, Freda and Benny were furniture shopping for their new home. "Freda!" Benny shouted. "Look at this wardrobe – it's beautiful. We've got to have it!"

About The Author

Deborah Fox lives in Yorkshire with her partner, Paul. She currently works for a large electrical distributor, as well as being a budding author.

Like many children, Deborah spent her time inspired by stories from AA Mile to JM Barrie, and to this day her favourite story is still *Winnie the Pooh*! Her writing talents didn't materialise until later in life, as most of her childhood was spent dancing and performing.

Deborah's passions are the outdoors, gardening, interior design, dogs, and cinema. She has always been intrigued with all things supernatural and the time presented to her during COVID, and the inspiration from the sad passing of her dog, Jake, was the start of her first novel: *Second Hand Rose.*

With the support of family, friends, and Blossom Spring agreeing to publish her story, it has fulfilled Deborah's dream to become a published author, and has given her the encouragement to write more stories.

www.blossomspringpublishing.com

Printed in Great Britain
by Amazon